In the Times of Love And Longing

Amrita Pritam

Imroz

HIND POCKET BOOKS

An imprint of Penguin Random House

HIND POCKET BOOKS

USA | Canada | UK | Ireland | Australia
New Zealand | India | South Africa | China | Singapore

Hind Pocket Books is part of the Penguin Random House group of companies whose addresses can be found at global.penguinrandomhouse.com

Published by Penguin Random House India Pvt. Ltd
4th Floor, Capital Tower 1, MG Road,
Gurugram 122 002, Haryana, India

First published in Hind Pocket Books by Penguin Random House India 2021

10 9 8 7 6 5 4 3 2

The views and opinion expressed in this book are the aurhor's own and the facts are as reported by her which have been verified to the extent possible, and the publishers are not in any way liable for the same.

ISBN 9789353490225

Printed at Manipal Technologies Limited, India

www.penguin.co.in

MIX
Paper | Supporting responsible forestry
FSC® C043100

This is a legitimate digitally printed version of the book and therefore might not have certain extra finishing on the cover.

HIND POCKET BOOKS

In the Times of Love And Longing

Amrita Pritam was an Indian maverick writer and poet. She is considered the first eminent female Punjabi writer, novelist and poet of the 20th century. Her writing is equally loved by the people of India and Pakistan. In her over 6 decades long career, she produced over hundred works, including poetry, essays, novels, biographies, etc. She was honoured with prestigious awards like the 'Sahitya Akademi,' 'Bharatiya Jnanpith,' and 'Padma Vibhushan' among many others.

Imroz is a famous Painter. He met Amrita through an artist when she was looking for someone to design the cover of her book. Trapped in a loveless marriage at a young age, Amrita Pritam dared to love – lyricist Sahir Ludhianvi at first, and artist Imroz later. While her first love remained unfulfilled, she spent the rest of her life living-in with a rather loving and caring Imroz.

Introduction

This book tells a love story.

A love story told through the letters exchanged between Amrita Pritam, the renowned author and poet, and her long-time companion Imroz, the artist. A relationship between words and colours.

The reader can get intimate glimpses of their extraordinary relationship that flowered for more than forty five years and in many ways, it still continues to blossom in its own unique manner.

Imroz believes and often reiterates: "How can Amrita be dead, when I am alive? We shared and continue to share many beautiful moments. Amrita is still alive in my being."

When she met Imroz, Amrita was a mother of two. Much older to Imroz. She was into a loveless marriage. Imroz was a bachelor and a struggling artist.

When and how this professional interaction turned into love, we do not know.

History has it that the two loved each other and withstood all opposition with courage and conviction. The passion they shared saw them through.

Imroz devoted all his life to Amrita. The ritual of marriage never fascinated him. In Amrita he found his love, who had been disillusioned with her marriage. He did not want her to go through the ritual again. He never had children, because Amrita was a mother of two and her children became 'ours', he claims with the pride of a father.

He believes that when you love someone, you just accept the

person in totality. He accepted Amrita without an argument. According to him, "A person in love never says why. A lover accepts everything about the beloved unconditionally."

The letters in this book reflect the love that these two extraordinary people shared.

Together they – the writer and the artist – lived in a world of colours, thoughts, words and poems. Amrita's career as a writer blossomed and she became a legend in Punjabi Literature. Imroz, though equally talented, chose to remain behind her like a shadow that would never let her feel alone.

These letters reflect their yearnings for each other and the evolution of their relationship.

Ms. Arvinder, the translator, a Punjabi poet, has commendably translated and presented the letters to the readers in English.

As editor of the book, Ms. Uma Trilok, a long time friend of Amrita and Imroz, in her note, provides the backdrop of an emotional imagery – a mix of visual, situational and emotional context to the letters.

Translator's Note

As I see, translation is rendering of an original text into another language. It generally carries a bicultural and a bilingual tone. This linguistic-cultural tradition is quite forcefully suggested in the target language. Hence some concessions have to be made for a degree of awkwardness in this rendering, if at all.

A translation has to be true to the original and yet it cannot and should not be the original. The translation has to convey the existence of the other language – *Punjabi* in this case. It has to take the reader along with the original text, even if it is a language which he does not understand.

In translation, some flavour of the original is lost. But in parts, some gets added.

However, in this translation, an effort has been made that the emotional expressions of both Amrita and Imroz are retained just as they were, for readers to savour as if from the original.

At other places, the intensity of their emotions has been expressed without even breaking it with their signatures.

Some letters in the book are additional notes to the letters, carrying the main letter further. There are no addresses. There are no signatures. These are letters within letters which are perhaps to express diverse thoughts within the same envelop.

Readers will note that some letters have been signed by Aashi, others by Ami and yet some by Amrita. Many other letters have also been signed by Maja. These are some endearments used for Amrita by Imroz.

Ima, Imma, Imva and Jeeti are some of the names which Amrita used for Imroz.

Arvinder

Arvinder teaches English at Govt. College For Girls, Chandigarh. She is multi-lingual. She writes in English as well as in Punjabi and Hindi. She is the author of a book of Punjabi poetry. She has also translated a book on Memory Improving Methods into English. Currently she is working on a project on writing skills in English.

Editor's Note

"Bombay welcomes its artist" was the one line letter that was received by Imroz from Amrita. He had then gone to Mumbai for work, leaving his job in Delhi.

The letter was just a line. It did not carry any name – his or hers. He was overwhelmed.

"Bombay was just an extension of Amrita, a reflection of her existence," he thought.

Amrita was more than a person for Imroz. She reflected many lacets for him.

Imroz used many endearments for Amrita. He still does.

From Ashi to Barkate – there have been so many. For him whatever denoted beauty, love, strength, compassion in the world, symbolised and still symbolises Amrita.

After reading 'Zobra the Greek' he started calling her 'Zorbi'. When he read 'The Naked Maja', a novel based on the life story of a Spanish artist, he started calling her ‚Maja'. Somehow he found this name to be sweet, warm and personal. It was much later that he came to know that ‚Maja' in Marathi can be translated as 'mine'. Perhaps that is why this name was so close to his heart.

While I was doing my book on their love relationship (Amrita-Imroz – A love story, Penguin) I often heard Imroz addressing Amrita as 'Barkate' – which means opulence. It has special significance in Punjab when used in the kitchen. She was actually abundance incarnate for him. Being self-employed, Imroz had his financial ups and downs but with Amrita around, he never felt deprived. His frugal fare blossomed into plenty with her touch.

Once they conversed till late - till about two in the night. Next morning she got up with a severe pain in her shoulder. She stayed in bed. He sat beside her. Suddenly she seemed charged with energy. It was sudden, like an epiphany. It was the idea of a book. She picked up some papers and started writing. Awestruck, he stared at her. She appeared fine. Bewildered and surprised, he got up and went to the kitchen. Offering her a cup of tea, he asked, "Whom do you resemble most?" "God", she replied casually. That day he realised, her name was 'God' too. But he never called her by that name. He had seen her, though, as a creator, when she worked. A creator saw another creator.

Amrita's ability to bounce back became evident whenever she called me for 'Reiki' healing. Once when she was invited to attend a book release, she was so unwell that it was difficult for her to move on her own. The organisers pleaded with her to attend the function. I was with her at that time. With some persuasion, she agreed to attend the function on the condition that I would go with her. I happily agreed. With great care I was able to take her to the Habitat Centre hall where the book was to be released. During the function, the organisers asked her to recite her famous poem *Waris Shah.* Reluctantly she agreed. But once she started the recitation, I was amazed to see and hear the passion, emotion, vigour and the energy that Amrita possessed. Her voice resonated in the hall like once I had heard during my college days.

In divergence to Amrita's variations and contrasts, I found Imroz a very simple and calm ocean of love and understanding. He seemed unaffected by the happening around him. His smile, love for life, and energy levels were unaffected, be it while he was being creative with colours or in the kitchen. While narrating his pleasant or unpleasant experiences, sharing his life's philosophy or while observing flowers, he calmly accepted life without question. Yet, he pursued his dreams earnestly. Materialism is alien to him. His silence seems to say, "Being *sehaj,* in turbulent times, is divine."

Amrita once wrote to Imroz: "Imroz my love, my dream! My entire life is a missive. Every beat of the heart is like a word; each breath a continuation; each day a sentence and all my life an epistle. If this epistle had reached you, I would never have needed the crutches of words or language." This was the extent of the intensity of her love for Imroz.

Apart from the letters printed here, several of her works are in the form of letters.

Sunehre is a long poem that began with the receipt of a letter from Sahir Ludianwi – a famous Urdu poet and lyrist, whom she loved before she met Imroz.

Imroz was working for Urdu dailies *Shamma and Aaina* when *Aakhri khat,* a poem-letter written by her to Sahir came to be published in *Aaina.* Imroz asked Amrita, "For whom have you written this letter? If you tell me, I will make a sketch of that person." Amrita blushed.

In yet another poem-letter *Ik khat,* the entire earth writes and people read.

A poem, *Ehadnaama* (a promise), is also a letter.....a treaty of peace in which she calls upon the people of this world to come and sign. It was written at a time when the Indo-Pak treaty was being signed at Tashkent.

Her poem *Sal Mubarak* was also a poem-letter for Imroz, which she wrote in January 1961, during their brief estrangement. She just sent the poem. There was no letter with it.

The cold frost of long lonely years, which Amrita spent before Imroz came into her life, melted with the warmth of his love for her. The crimson colour that surrounded Amrita's persona was the reflection of Imroz's love for her.

Amrita did not hesitate in expressing her yearning for love. She longed for a lover like Imroz. No amount of praise or adulation helped to satisfy her. A word from her lover alone was what she repeatedly desired. Imroz turned out to be the answer to her quest.

Before Imroz entered Amrita's life, she suffered the personal pangs of separation through her characters which she created in her stories and novels. This is reflected when she put a question to Imroz about one of her character in her novel, "Will Sundara meet the same fate every time in every age?" This reflects the state of her personal agony at that moment.

Imroz wove the dreams for her afresh. Unlike Sahir Ludhianvi, Imroz gave her a solid soil to dream on, build and live. Throughout her life, Amrita drank from the fragrance of Imroz's love. When away, his letters lit the fire of passion in her heart which she has very vividly expressed in her letters to him. His love sustained her. Her pining for Sahir's love was a prelude to her passion for Imroz.

Amrita never wanted to be a hurdle in the way of Imroz's career, yet she continued to call out his name loudly, calling him sometimes a Mirza or a Ranjha.

For half a century, Amrita wrote love songs but lovelorn as she was, she wanted someone to call out her name lovingly. *"Sun mere bandhu, Sun mere mitwa"* she empathised with.

Amrita knew she was Imroz's conscious choice but she was also aware of her own compulsions. She was very conscious of her age – she was seven years older than him. Imroz, though, did not want her to measure her age in time but with the intensity of his love for her. The transitory nature of life Amrita talked about, and her response to it, had been of chasing life gone by. She wanted to enjoy each moment of life left with him.

On foreign trips, Amrita missed Imroz all the more. Be it while enjoying sea waves or sharing Henry Miller's writings, she wanted him to be close by.

When she was not with him, she lived with his memory. She sometimes slept with it, woke up with it, and continued her conversation with him.

Imroz for Amrita was not perfect because the word perfect she felt was stale and cold; instead, she found the word 'progress' more akin to him – leaving something behind each day and finding something new.

Amrita responded to love fervently. Love, according to her, had the potency to produce a bright future even from a barren present. Amrita was a great lover of nature, savoured its beauty and expressed it in her works as well as in her letters to him. She loved flowers; she cherished them as gifts from friends. She described situations and instances associated with them, with great relish.

It is amazing that very few readers know that the strength behind Amrita's success was Imroz. His love and companionship gave strength and vigour to her creativity. She compared his love for her to the life-force, she received from him which she utilised—we all know, to create such massive and meaningful literature.

She was consciously elated by the fact that both Imroz and she shared the same earth and lived under the same sky.

The collection of letters that are being presented here are the personal passion of Amrita and Imroz.

The letters traverse the terrain of a very sensitive and intense relationship.

Uma Trilok

Note

While collecting from Amrita letters for publication, which she had written to Imroz, she had said, "Look here Imroz! This information is incomplete. Can you recall that while writing the preface to a book on Kafka's beloved Arthur Councilor wrote 'I have got Kafka's letters, but without Melina's letters, Kafka's portrait is incomplete. ' He used to say that Melina's letters are like 'drops of rain on my scorched head' and that 'he has lost these drops of rain'. But thank God! I have your letters with me which I can lend for the book. "

The compilation of the same is being presented..

from imroz

1

Your expression is simply beautiful! And your thoughts are out of this world. Fears and apprehensions do not go well with you. I can't bear to see you like that. You can never be afraid of anything. And then I am always there with you. Listen to me and you will realise that the more you broaden your trust, the smaller your fears shall become. Do not measure your age in units of time please! Why can't you measure it with my desires. Embrace my intensity and the beating of my heart. My desires, my longings are your age and my intensity your health.

You are trying to leave your past behind. You are in pain, I know.

This pain is temporary. Come into the future! The future is smiling at you and waiting at its threshold with open arms and a throbbing heart.

Waiting for destiny.

Bombay, 2nd October, 1959 Your future Jeeti

from imroz 2

My universe!

My devotion!

I bow to you!

The moment I bow before you, I feel the nine hundred mile long desert that separates us, suddenly fades into oblivion.

As long as you are my destiny, I am not scared of any misfortune.

Bombay, 24th October, 1959 *Your Jeeti*

from imroz

3

Aashi,

Heartfelt wishes to destiny on our first Diwali! And all the others who are our own.

You are my treasure, look after yourself.

Do not bury my treasure under the weight of sadness. This is unfair. See how strong I am! I am struggling with an indifferent livelihood in an alien land.

I do not think negatively, it is not in my disposition and I cannot bend in the face of difficulties.

All roads of my life are difficult – the one on which I met you, is also replete with difficulties, but that is how our life is.

For how long shall the difficulties stare us in the face?

We are brave and our steps are strong, and fast. We are the children of destiny.

Your Jeeti would never want to be defeated.

Bombay, 29th October, 1959

from imroz

4

Such touching and beautiful letters Jeeti!

More beautiful than anything that I have ever been able to imagine. I waited for such letters all my life. This wait never became a reality but I kept writing replies to these letters. Many of my poems are replies to such unreceived letters. And today, they have become a reality and I am overwhelmed, almost beyond myself. Tears keep welling my eyes as I think of life. It really seems to have passed by. Why didn't the years of my life stop to see and feel this incredible truth? Why is time still passing? Today my age is unable to match up to yours.

You are calling me to an enchanted land, a magical valley, but time is still adding years to my age. My heart and my age pull me in different directions. There is this pull at the heartstrings and there is this dilemma of my declining years. My heart stopped – spellbound – the moment you beckoned. Now it seems many years are passing within a single day. I am not able to carry the weight of time anymore.

from imroz

5

My love!

Just tell me once that you want to be with me. My destiny! I am just waiting for a nod from you. Time is waiting for you, my present, my future is waiting for you.

My life is at your disposal.

Love, just call me once.

7.30 evening

from imroz

6

I am writing this letter from the house of destiny! If you are the wick, I am the spark, but we do not spread brightness. Let us come together and brighten ourselves and brighten our lives. A day will come when all our numerous prayers would be answered. Amen!

12th November, 1959 Jeeti

from imroz

7

Do not count the days of my absence. I have taken up a house at a beautiful place, come and make it a home – your home and a home of our dreams. For the first time in life, I have desired a home. When we met, you were so inaccessible. Trust me a little more, trust my love. I would be with you till all the limits of life. All my past, present and future belong to you.

Jeeti

from imroz

8

Don't lose hope, Aashi! I am coming. Do not see the reflection of hope in the broken mirror of the past. See it in the full and bright mirror of the future. Throw aside the pieces of broken trust and look at me with all your heart. My entire universe is waiting for you. Just for you...

This is my first day in an alien land, first step on this road. I have taken this first step with all my heart. I want to evolve a different style in my work, a reflection of my inner self. Come with me and be all my courage, my art and my enthusiasm. Hold the hand of my trust and let us bridge the gap of these nine hundred miles. I am with you in every breath. This temporary separation would brighten and deepen the colours of our love.

With this trust – yours

Rajan is a sensitive character – a lover – in one of Amrita's novel 'Aashu'. It was after having read 'Aashu' that Imroz called Amrita for the first time. The reference in the following letter is also to this incident.

---

from imroz

9

My destiny! Rajan did not exist on this earth. He was the man of my dreams. The day you called, after reading *Aashu,* 'I am your Rajan', the dream became a reality. It took my heart away in a single breath. It is sheer benevolence as well as a strange quirk of fate. A cold frost of long, lonely years that had settled on me melted with the warmth of your gaze. And now after having sent you nine hundred miles away, that frost is filling my being all over again. I am deeply aware of the circumstances that have forced you to go away. This feeling is my consolation, a shelter against the frost of your separation. It would help me survive. And when the wait is over, you would come and look at me again and my inner being shall blossom into its true crimson colour.

21st January, 1960 Your Begum

from imroz

10

Got a beautiful letter from a beautiful woman.

A charming message from a charmer.

This letter is my pride.

You are the beautiful illusion of my life and a beautiful reality too.

26th January, 1960

from imroz

11

I was happy yesterday but today I am very sad.

I feel like leaving everything here to just be with you and to never be anywhere without you.

Life without you is a punishment. Who wants to undergo punishment while life is around?

If ever I get engrossed in work, severe depression sets in. Once the work is over, I ask, why am I here?

Why am I without you? I am angry at myself. Extremely angry.

Yours,

Yours only.

from imroz

12

My faith, my anchor!

The spark in my pen has blossomed into a bright flame with your presence in my life. This flame received floral tribute in Nepal yesterday and I showered all the flowers on the altar of your remembrance.

‚A faint light is flickering through the dark night of separation...'

The bright flame of your remembrance burnt in this poem that I wrote. This flame of love was being discussed till late last night. So many love poems in Nepali, Hindi and Bangla came alive.

There was a couplet in Persian. Its essence was: 'We chase illusions and run after mirages'.

We long and pine for some water, but there is just sand in the desert of life. Some wise people know the truth of mirages and abandon the chase. They must be wise, surely. But I strongly feel that those who do not mistake the sand for water, their own desire, their thirst, their longing must be incomplete in some way. Perhaps they have not yearned intensely enough. Honestly my love, I do not want this wisdom. I am happy to celebrate my longing even though it makes me wander in deserts all my life.

May all my sweet remembrance reach you.

My love, my Jeeti, my mirage!

Kathmandu, 27th January, 1960 Aashi

from imroz

13

My love,

You met me now, now, when my life has reached its evening. This journey is about to come to an end. If destiny willed our coming together, then perhaps we should have met when life exuded the warmth of youth. As they say, it was the noon of life. You could have felt its warm sunshine. In Kathmandu, someone read this poem in Hindi.

At heart, human beings share the same pain, the same anguish, wherever they might live on earth. I think all of us feel the same wrench, the same pull at the heartstrings. In the cold evening of life, I now wait just for the warm sunshine that your letters bring... Just yours.

The walls of your city (Bombay) are harsh and cruel. My tender feelings get bruised and hurt against these walls. I have already spent fourteen long years of exile from my love – like the exile of Ram. It seems the remaining years too would be spent in the same longing.

I have received just one letter from you. Have you forgotten my Kathmandu address? Each day I wait, just for a word from you. People here have told me so much about my writing, in very touching words...But all the praise that was showered on me only aggravated my longing for you. I am burning in the fire of my passion and am unable to endure any longer. I have been waiting eagerly for the past three days and now a fever has caught me.

I returned yesterday from Kathmandu, had to change the flight, as I could not get a reservation in the direct flight. Reached here after nine at night.

My craving still expected a message, a word from you. Why have you become so frugal with your words!

Even today, the postman went by my door without stopping.

You told me once that you were the answer to all my questions. Isn't it strange that you are so silent now!

1st February, 1960

from imroz

14

My love,

I do not feel like going anywhere or meeting anyone.

My restless eyes look at the door again and again, maybe there is a letter from you.

But no!

Heard your voice on the radio in the evening and was a little satisfied that you have come. Maybe something has happened in Nepal.

You have not written at all...

2nd February, 1960

from imroz

15

My sweetheart,

You are the manifestation of my future!

Why don't you say something? Say something, even though you are angry.

Just order me once. Just say once. I can sacrifice anything and everything.

You are my passion! My obsession!

Put my reality to test at least!

I am living just to see the beauty and all the smiles of the world on your lips.

Yours, only yours...

3rd February, 1960

from imroz

16

Just got your letter – a message from the queen of my heart.

I was going to post all my letters that I wrote to you everyday. Just read them once. After that, say whatever you feel like.

Do not be sad. Don't get annoyed.

On the 25th I had written a long letter to you while you were in Nepal. But I think that did not reach you, otherwise you would not have thought the way you did.

I don't know if you are my dusk, my dawn or my noon but you are my destination, my destiny. I have felt this many times over, and feel it now too as if I have done a wrong to my queen by coming to Bombay.

This thought disappoints me and I find everything disgusting -my work, my talent, everything. You might compare yourself to a beautiful evening but do not forget you are my morning too and even my noon. Just live and see! With all your heart and with me, with your own Jeeti.

3rd February, 1960

from imroz 17

You breathe life into my songs! A letter from you reached me today. I am grateful to life that it has brought back the replies to my letters. But why haven't you received all of mine? This is the seventh one that I am writing. I wrote three before leaving for Nepal and one I wrote on that fateful day...the day you, my peace, went nine hundred miles away. And I kept writing every day after that.

I had written once with a heart that was full to the brim. 'The letter of life drifted, destiny could not read the name of my beloved on it, I wrote the name in my blood'... But now that the name is known, it appears circumstances have conspired with my destiny and no one is able to read the name....

I read a song by Tagore in Nepal:

You are my ocean, you are my sailor
I am a boat
Why should I look for the shores?
If I drown, I shall drown in you.
You are my ocean.

The poem consoled me.

5th February, 1960 Yours Aashi

from imroz

18

Khrushchev was invited to lunch by Pt. Jawaharlal yesterday.

I went there.

I like Pandit ji. He epitomizes all that is beautiful in humanity.

I was very happy for a while but all of a sudden the fact of being away from you seized me intensely and everything became meaningless – the days, the routine, the socialising – everything.

13th February, 1960 Aashi

from imroz

19

It is past midnight, almost 2 o'clock and I am feeling impoverished.

You, the wealth of my life, is not with me.

Would you ever understand this?

My treasure! Come!

Let us spend the wealth of life together.

16th February, 1960 Jeeti

from imroz 20

You were to come on the eighteenth but you did not.

It was as if the sun did not rise that morning. It is my destiny after all and that of the Sun, why should you be bothered!

Like me, Sundra, Puran's beloved also said one day.

"He went to the woods and never returned, Jogis can never be true friends." Will Sundra meet the same fate, every time in every age!

No one can change the course of destiny, Jeeti!

I cleaned your room yesterday. Wiped the mirror in the hope to see the reflection of my fate in it.

"Dreams can be fostered afresh", your words are haunting me, echoing in my ears and then they turn into an unbearable, terrible noise that may drive me insane!

But no! I shall build the palace of your new dreams even on the ruins of my life. I will try that even a faint sigh of mine may not mingle into the breeze of your city.

Not a trace of my pain be an obstacle in the way of your progress....

Unfortunate Aashi

from imroz

21

I can't live a borrowed life any more!

Destiny has played many deceptive games with us and now it's our turn to play with destiny.

You call yourself an evening. Do you know what a beautiful evening you are? Come let us celebrate and live this evening with all our heart and soul and body and with all our creative talent.

"Unfortunate Aashi" is my destiny, my fortune.

If you are a beautiful evening then I shall live this evening with all my strength, my vitality and with the intense warmth of my noon.

We shall live it.

Time might stare from a distance or might just come along with us, but we shall live and live more beautifully than ever.

With this promise and with this trust.

19th February, 1960 Yours Jeeti

from imroz

22

Mirza! Come back to your Neeli* and to your Sahiba too!

So much of our life has been spent in longing. Let the remaining days not pass in waiting to be together. Let miracles happen, Mirza! Come and rewrite destiny while there is still time.

Had a slight fever a day before. It worsened yesterday. At night I was very restless.

I am reminded of a couplet by Jigar:

Is drja bekrar the dard-e-niha se hm,
Kuch door aage barh gye umr-e-rvan se hm

Oh love, come to me! Should I lend my wings to you! My darling, I shall not get this cheque encashed. But I just want the wealth of love. Let me see how generous life is!

21st February, 1960 Yours Aashi

* Neeli was the name of the first car that they bought. It was also the name of the mate of Mirsa, the legendary lover.

from imroz

23

No letter from you sweetheart!

I accept whatever you want to give me.

Let me accept this as well, I am not waiting for your letters.

I am waiting for you.

What did you say "misfortune"?

Misfortune comes very easily, and you do not come even after such long wait and earnest requests.

Misfortune comes on its own, even without calling, but you do not come at all.

So I think you are not misfortune, you are my good fortune.

22nd February, 1960 Jeeti

from imroz

24

I talked to you on the telephone with the idea that it would give me some peace but I have become all the more restless.

I am not interested in anything.

The house is silent and vacant. It stares emptily back at me. I detach myself from myself and rush towards you and when I am not able to reach you, I grapple with myself and become more restless.

I have to earn a livelihood but I am not able to work with all my heart. In fact, my heart is not with me. Someone has taken it away and is now sitting, silently somewhere.

Can't you feel my agony?

My restlessness?

Does it make you happy?

Are you doing this deliberately?

Why do we become obsessive like this? Why?

But how are you concerned? You are patience personified or should I call you an incarnation of silence!

You do not even write to me! How are you concerned? Some one may just go insane for you!

All right, just come to me once then I shall face all misfortunes. If you come to me, I shall never have any complaints about destiny or about time.

It is impossible to live without you. Do you want to drive me totally insane?

Why are you wasting the noon of your life in waiting? Why don't you simply live it?

Do you love the pain of separation? Your poetry cannot survive without it? These poems immersed in melancholy have brought you so much of fame.

You are on a high pedestal. You cannot live without this adulation now but can you live without life?

Why do we live a life which is more of a curse!

All right! Whenever you find time from your poetry call me!

Whatever I have for you and for life, I shall present you.

Would you be there by the evening of life?

At least try and live the evening.

I am almost driven insane and you are lost in your world of poetry.

Let us see what happens when you too get driven to this brink of insanity.

And till then I salute my poetess!

21st February, 1960 In madness, Jeeti

from imroz

25

Such a delicate and tender letter!

It had the fragrance of your love. I drank deep at this fragrance several times.

Sethi's* phone disturbed me. When he heard my voice, he said, "You sound happy, today" and I told him "I have just received his letter. I think my voice is reflecting it." He had a good laugh.

Honestly, it has come like a ray of light in the long night of separation.

Such a loving, sweet letter – it has lit the fire of passion afresh.

Just want you here with me, living, throbbing – whether you come out of the earth or descend from the heavens!

22nd February, 1960 Forever yours-Aashi

---

* Narinder Sethi, a fellow artist and a friend.

from imroz

26

My destiny!

If you don't get a train reservation, book a flight please!

Do not think about the money – I will pay the rest of it.

I am not in love with melancholy.

I long for that ultimate destination of love. It was to tread this arduous path that I write songs of melancholy. They have sustained me during the ordeal of your separation.

I don't love the fame that has come my way through these songs. I long for life that is filled with your love.

You are my destination.

Come and measure your insanity with mine!

I feel the fourteen years that I have spent pining for Sahir's love were just a prelude to my passion for you.....

Your Own-Aashi

from imroz

27

My life is for you – entirely at your disposal.

You may live it, use it or just be indifferent to it.

But you certainly cannot blame me.

My art is your wealth, you are free to spend it, be extravagant. Take away the years in my life – I cannot bear their intensity, each moment is yours.

You seem to be an incarnation of patience!

Why not have a feel of my impatience and my restlessness for a while.

22nd February, 1960 Yours Jeeti

from imroz

28

It will soon be evening and I have been waiting for you.

Your letter has not come.

Is everything all right?

You protect the hues of my hopes! Take care that these bright colours do not fade.

Just see, I have lost everything else while trying to find these colours and now these are totally yours.

I am ecstatic at my good fortune of having won over my colours.

I have no regrets, what I lost in the bargain.

You are god's gift to me.

Wait for me, and keep me informed, of each and every moment of the well being of these colours of life.

The one who belongs to you and colours.

24th April, 1960 Jeeti

29

from imroz

My darling Jeeti!

On my request, just go to your bedroom now, switch on the radiogram and listen to Burman's voice: *Sun mere bandhu re, Sun mere mitva...* (Listen my friend. O listen to me my dear).

Where are the people whom someone calls with such longing? I spent my life writing love poems but I know it very clearly that I would not be called by anyone like this. And I also know that you are the one whom I am calling and that no reply shall ever reach me.

Yesterday, a dream like letter of yours arrived.

I know the conflict of your mind. Although I am your conscious choice but my age and my compulsions, my worldly bonds are your conflict.

When I looked at you and heard your voice, I stopped. Your presence filled my being with happiness.

Peace descended and I stopped wandering in the maze of the world and relationships.

But you are denying me everything now.

Do I still have to live in this world where I am not a part of your life, your imagination and your dream!

Hearing your footsteps, I had told life.....'listen carefully.....listen to the soft sound of footsteps.... Do not close your doors'.

But today I am unable to hear the sound of your footsteps.

What should I ask from life now?

Shall I tell her to close all doors.....

26th April, 1960

from imroz
30

My love, my world!

I am not going anywhere.

I don't want to go anywhere without you. What would I do with all this fame from across the seas?

I wrote those poems for you and if they are not acceptable to you, the praise that comes from strangers has no meaning.

There is a song in Gujarati that says "precious pearls of wisdom abound but the city of the heart remains desolate".

There are so many philosophies to console but honestly, I am lonely without you.

Every time I have to fill up the passport form, its columns stare at me.* I just cannot fill the lines that hurt you, and make you unhappy.

I live for you, my life is for you.

I shall not go anywhere. Just wait for you to come back to me.

27th April, 1960 Your Aashi

---

* The lines relate to the following instance: Amrita while filling up a form for a visa, could not face the harsh realities that came to her mind when she came to filling the section where she had to give details of her spouse. She tore the form in frustration.

from imroz

31

Mistress of my soul!

I am giving all that I have to you, rather to your distrust.

I am ripping away all my passions, all my desires from this city and sewing all of them with your city, your desires and your happiness with my trust and with your distrust!

I would be coming soon, but I don't know when that illusive trust shall come...

29th April, 1960 Your Jeeti

Amrita at her desk.

A portrait of Amrita in 1965

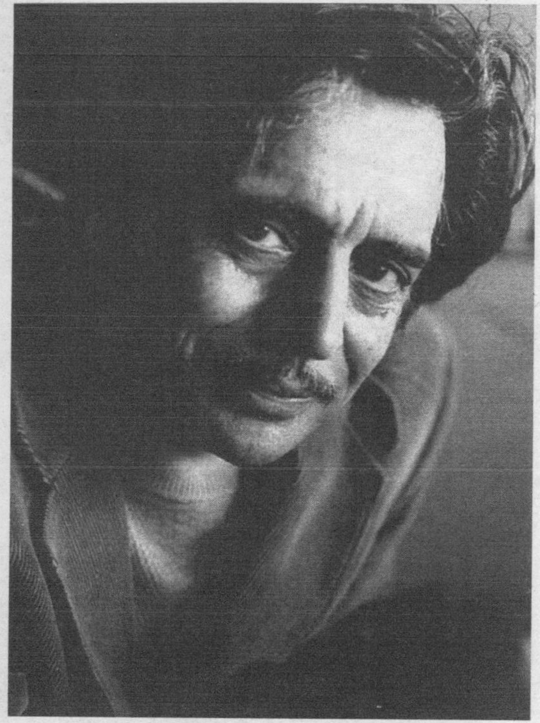

A portrait of Imroz (around 1965)

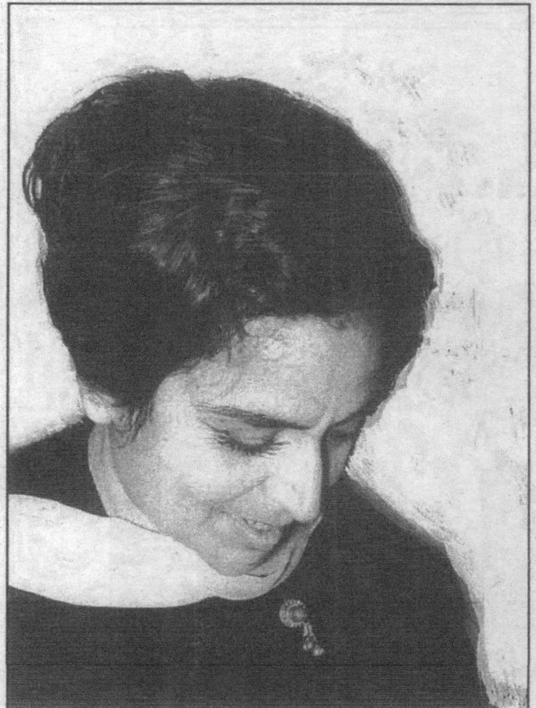
Amrita in 1975

Imroz in reflective mood in 2001

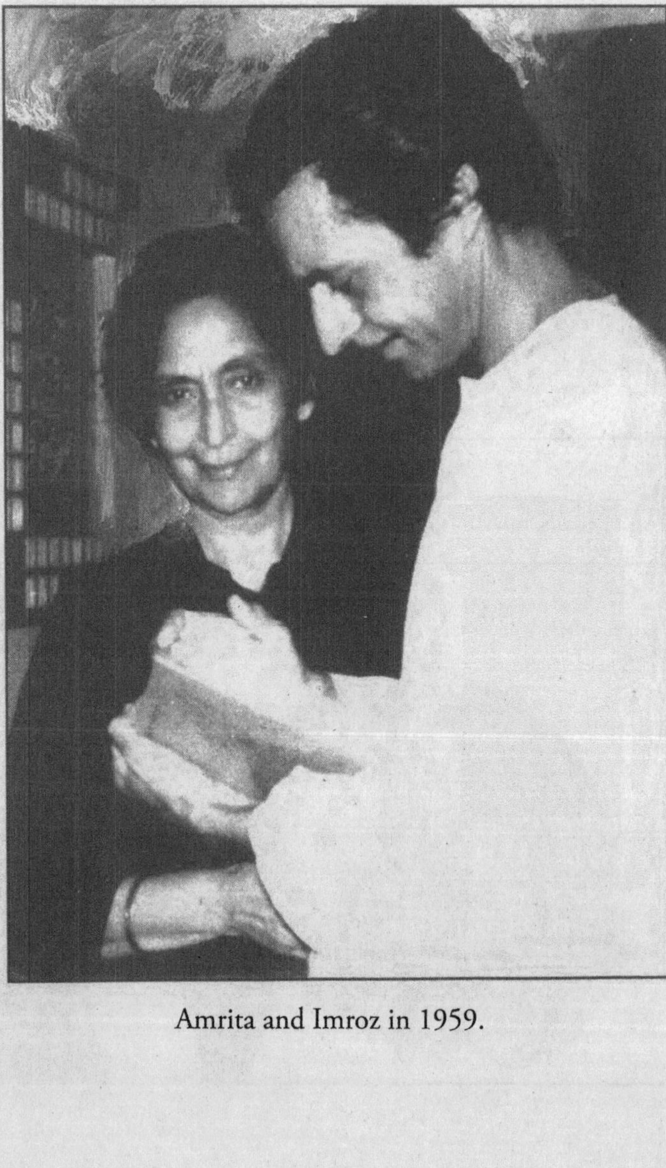

Amrita and Imroz in 1959.

Amrita and Imroz, in the 1990's.

At a temple in Himachal Pradesh in 1958.

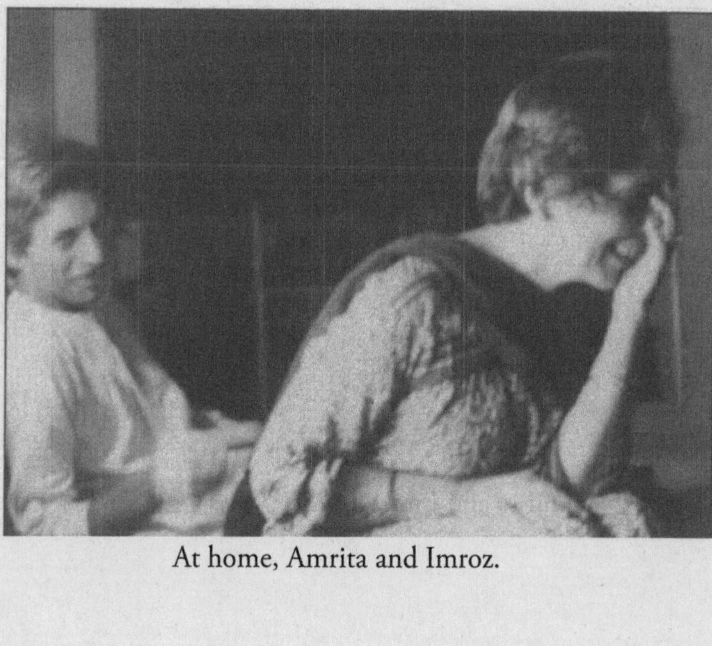

At home, Amrita and Imroz.

Amrita with her veena at All India Radio,
Lahore before the Partition.

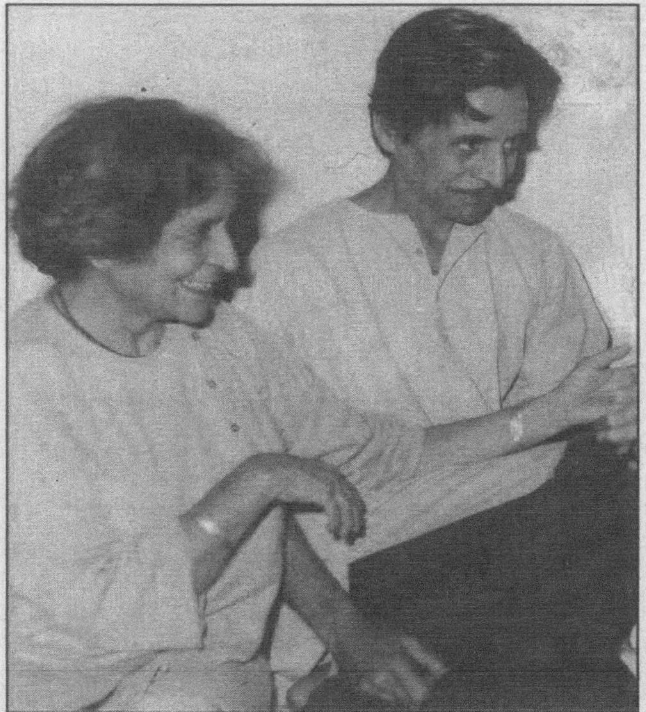

At home in a light-hearted mood.

Amrita and Imroz outside a temple.

At her desk in the 1960's

from imroz

32

My Jeeti!

Jeevi* has become a part of my inner self – vibrant and beautiful, enjoying a swing ride in gay abandon. Suddenly, she sees a face and falls under its spell – totally hypnotised. Destiny had shown a face to her but she was utterly oblivious of the hardships that were in store for her. Jeevi followed him blindly. There was no direction for her. She was lost in a blind alley. The one, who was to be her savior, was lost somewhere in the crowd. Life had nothing to offer but bitterness.

Lost in the arduous paths of life, she was driven to insanity. Her beloved saw her wretchedness. He had earlier rejected her for the sake of society while she was in the full bloom of her youth but now, when she was insane, he held her hand and claimed her as his own in front of society, right in the face of all its obsolete and oppressing values.

Jeevi has become a part of my being. She is there in my writing, in my imagination and in my reality. My dear Jeeti, I think the day I go insane the way Jeevi did – perhaps that day you would come to me – with the same determination with which you held my hand one day and took me to buy an engagement ring. There would be

---

* Those days Amrita was translating a Gujarati novel Jeevi. The reference in this letter is to this character Jeevi.

the same warmth once again, the same passion and the same sanctity of feeling.

26th April, 1960 Despairing Aashi

Let the joys and sorrows of life – yours and mine – mingle like waters from two rivers. And then, it would be difficult to separate your existence from mine just as no one can draw a line on water.

29th April, 1960 Always praying for your long life

from imroz

33

My destiny! My queen!

I am coming to you! This Thursday itself.

On 5th of May, in the morning at ten, I shall reach your city.

Be ready, my Sahiba! I shall bring you back with me, in my Neeli, forever and I shall always look after you.

My noon shall mingle with your evening and you shall become even more beautiful, and more exquisite.

Just wait for one day more.

Only one day.

We have waited for three long years – long like a life time.

3rd May, 1960 All yours, Jeeti

from imroz

34

On the 8th of May, 1960, Amrita and Imroz went to Bombay in their first blue car - Neeli. The first night they stopped in Gwalior and the second in Indore. Those days Amrita thought Navtej was her closest friend. So she wanted to share her happiness with him first. That night at Lantern hotel in Indore, Amrita wrote a letter to Navtej. The original letter is still with Navtej. The letter was written on the night of 9th of May, 1960.

Dear Navtej!

The year 1953 had posed a question: Life is an unending desert of separation – nine hundred miles long and vast.

Now in 1960, I have dared to cross the desert. On the eighth of this month, the distance started shrinking. Nine hundred miles changed into eight, eight into seven, seven into six, six into five, five into four, and today on the ninth, the distance is reduced to three hundred.

The distance of nine hundred miles made me write *'Sunehre', 'Aakhri Khat', 'Ek Sural' and 'Kasturi'.*

The other day, I was reading, Hemingway's *'The Old man and the sea'.* After wandering and starving for eighty four days, the sailor says, "Today, on the eighty fifth day, can't I buy a piece of good fortune?" Like the sailor, I want to say that now, it is my right to buy my piece of fortune too. I have paid for it through eighty four days of wandering and hunger. Have I not paid for it by writing *'Sunehre', 'Aakhri Khat', 'Ik Swal and Kasturi'?*

Now I have acquired the right to cross these miles.

I feel Darji has been with me to wet my parched lips in this desert. His words fall like raindrops on the sands of my soul. Please tell him I shall always treasure them. In this dessert my first letter is for you and Darji.

Lantern Hotel, 9th May, 1960 Yours Amrita

from imroz

35

Listen!

To love somebody is not just a strong feeling, it is also a decision, a judgment....

Even today I can talk only to you and to no one else.

I am telling you that I am extremely restless. No one else can understand. Although my voice is inaudible to you now but you are the only one for me.

I have a right on you – but all this is meaningless now, lifeless like this missive.

3rd Novmber, 1960

I vividly recall all those nights, those days, you and me, everything that you said, all my precious treasures, those sacred moments.

I did not know they would take away so much from me – the meaning of my existence, my manliness, my peace, my enthusiasm for life – just everything is lost. But I will not lose heart. I will not remain quiet. I will earnestly look for the one who has taken all this away – may be I have to go till the limit of courage, till the limit of sight, till the limit of imagination or even till the limit of life. I will try and find her and I am sure of my success.

The unfortunate one who is desperately seeking his good fortune. – Jeeti

from imroz

36

I am keeping your things carefully in the big black box.

I kept your sarees first and then your shirts and salwars, handkerchiefs, bangles, your files and all your stories and books of poems. And last of all three skeins of white wool and a half knit vest hanging in the knitting needles.

How I wish it could be completed. My life is incomplete too....

Your memory lingers and a few relics emerge.

There is still so much space in the trunk. I put both my hands in that incomplete vest and sat for a long time – weaving all my dreams in those unfinished threads.

This trunk had come to Bombay, filled to the brim with dreams to be realised...

Whenever you see my unfinished paintings, do have a good look at them – the moment your eyes fall on them, they become 'paintings', otherwise they are nothing but dead lines going from nowhere to nowhere.

4th November, 1960

37

from imroz

I am cleaning the studio.

Wiping your portrait, my hands stopped and I kept staring at the picture.

I was so proud of that portrait, but today the artist, the creator of the portrait, bowed before his own creation.

My eyes downcast – my pride bent, I cannot look into the eyes that stare at me from the picture.

But I wipe it everyday.

I revere it.

I worship it.

When shall my prayers be answered?

love!

14th November, 1960

from imroz

38

I had a very interesting dream last night.

You were making hot stuffed pranthas in the kitchen.

Shelley and I were sitting by your side.

Enjoying the breakfast.

You were very happy.

Since morning I have been just sitting around the room and thinking... could not eat anything at all... had eaten so much with your loving hands last night.

18th November, 1960

from imroz

39

My letters were powerless to bring you back.

I can understand your pain and your state of mind.

Aashi, I don't know why, but it is impossible for me to be without you.

I cannot live like this.

I have felt it strongly and I am sure about this.

Since the day I came away from you, I have not worked.

In fact, I am unable, powerless to work.

I cannot think anything without you. I cannot visualise life without you.

I am being consumed in a fire of my own... with the same belief and the same courage with which I had owned you up –

Yours Jeeti

I am watching you through the window of my imagination. You are silent, with eyes downcast.

You could talk about anything and everything to me when I was nobody to you. But now, when I think I mean so much to you, you are silent.

I was always yours.

I have come to the world just for you. But since a few days I have become a stranger.

This silence has fallen on my imagination like darkness. I am unable to see anything beyond it.

I am waiting for you to look at me once, lovingly, intently so that light returns in my life.

When my being and my imagination would be brightened...

My dear!

21st November, 1960 morning

40

from imroz

My love,

I cannot live in the silence of this darkness.

On Monday, the 28th of this month, I am coming to you in the morning at 10:30. I would then bring you – the light of my life, along with me.

I am lifeless and meaningless without you.

Whatever I might be, good or bad, I am all yours.

Whatever you are – you are all mine.

My treasure, my beautiful evening.

Wherever you are, count me along.

We are not going to be away from each other anymore, now – never!

21st November, 1960 Evening 4 O'clock Jeeti

from imroz

41

My love,

Life has taken you to a strange turn.

You are quiet, with me, with everything.

And now I am quiet with my own self.

I close my eyes, to see you Aashi – but now my eyes are not closing and I am unable to see anything.

I cannot see you as a stranger and I cannot see myself as a stranger.

23rd November, 1960

from imroz

42

My love,

The fault is mine.

I left you alone and came away.

This feeling of guilt is growing with each passing day.

May be even bigger than all your troubles - but.....

25th November, 1960

from imroz

43

Aashi, my love,

Your poems, your stories, your novels, your files, your sarees, your shirts, your bangles, your purse, your pictures, your Jeeti, incomplete knitting – all of us are coming to you.

On Thursday morning at 10.30 by the deluxe we shall reach New Delhi Station.

We shall all wait to see you – meet you.

Hope you would come to receive us yourself.

We would wait at the station, till you come.

Your Jeeti – who once was all yours, now perhaps a stranger – addresses you.

Before I came to Bombay, you had asked me to give you three days of my life – today it is my turn.

You may give me three days, three hours or three minutes – it is all up to you.

29th November, 1960

from imroz

44

My love,

You are the light in the night.

I am the darkness in the day.

You are the sacred vessel — I am damp wood.

The story of my defeat, the tomb of my passionate love, the robes of my heart full of thorns, everything, epitomizes my being.

I have read and carefully kept the tale of my defeat, the way I used to keep your affectionate letters and your pictures.

I could only make designs, but you have made a perfect picture of the tomb of love in that song that you have dedicated to me.

You can do everything in your writing.

You write so beautifully that it helps me to endure all the pain.

24th December, 1960

from imroz

45

During the beginning of 1961, besides some conventional letters, Amrita had sent a letter in the form of a story, "The sigh of the moon". This was followed by a poem 'Sal Mubarak' and Ayn Rand's novel 'The Fountain head'. Many of the 'letters' in this period were undated and unsigned.

Perhaps, mentioning of names and dates faded into the oblivion of sadness which she was experiencing during that time...

Jeeti!

Just see the difference of destinies!

Yours and mine.

You are the fortunate one – your beloved sacrificed everything for the sake of your love. You didn't even have to ask. And I am the unfortunate one – my beloved has closed his doors on me. My heart has matured and ripened with so much of pain of love and life. It doesn't get amused anymore by the frivolous rattles of hope.

Newspapers are writing about my days spent in Bombay almost every third day. The language is bitter, sarcastic and scathing. But I do not have any grudge against them. It is not within them to understand me and my values. What pains me more is the fact that you have not understood me, the man who told me once, "I am the answer to all your questions". Remember?

The mute bottles of paint lying in the drawer of your table know me better. I wipe them lovingly everyday. The colours look into my eyes and smile, because they have discovered the mysteries of my eyes. They know how passionate I am about your creative powers.

They crave for your touch because that alone justifies their existence. I crave for you because I discover the meaning of my existence in your creations. I experience this even in my own work. But with you around, it gets strengthened – bold and strong.

I am reminded of a very tender and special moment that had touched me so much. One day while you were working on your easel, I am not aware what my forehead asked of you. You unexpectedly, dipping your brush in colour, touched my forehead with it. Am I today suffering on account of that acceptance?

It is like the punishment that Adam got after he tasted the forbidden fruit. He was thrown out of paradise.

Another day, another time another letter

A Russian artist came to see me yesterday. He asked me to sit in front of him so that he could make my sketch. Perhaps no one can understand the pain of those moments for me. After he finished, I looked at the sketch. Tears welled up in my eyes. Perhaps the pencil also cried for your touch. Only your touch.

It wanted to be in your hands, just yours.

Regards to Faiz* - from an unfortunate woman who wrote his life story.

Another day, another time another letter

I received your letter. Jeeti dost,

* Artist Faiz of Bombay. Amrita's novel 'Bulava' is based on his life.

"I am not annoyed with you at all. Our meeting touched the limits of friendship. Friendship became love. Love turned into passion. As a person who has experienced this - how can I ever be annoyed with your

If this separation is a punishment, it is meant solely for me. This is not what I asked for. I had chosen love and togetherness. You chose to be away. Separation was your choice. It cannot be a punishment for you.

Your passion is pure. I have never doubted that. It is just that there is a youthful craving in it. You will have to cleanse it off – this craving, dear. We have seen it in its most terrible form. The way, you left me alone in a strangers house* — in fact, it was not the real you but that terrible craving within you.

I give you ten years.

Satisfy all your desires.

And, then with my lips I shall wipe away all the marks from your body and if you still want me. I will be ready to live with you and to die.....

---

* The reference is to Balwant Gargi's house. It was from here that they separated in November, 1960.

from imroz

46

You are annoyed with life.

My crime doesn't merit so much of punishment, love.

This is a bit too much.

This ten year long exile.....no please don't do this.

You have given life to me.......don't take it away now.

26th December, 1960

Your Jeeti

from imroz

47

The table and the drawer.

And....those bottles of colours wait...for that familiar loving touch everyday.

The touch that used to love them and made them shine.

That brush and those colours, still look for and wait for that face and that brow.

They still wait to adorn that brow that made them stay fresh otherwise they would have died by now.

Everyday I moisten them, with the water of your wait and do not let them go dry.

But their freshness is with you. You know that, freshness!

I am also waiting just for you – in my colours, in my life.

1st January, 1961 Jeeti

from imroz

48

Received both your letters.

Your poem in the first one - the poem of your agony and mine, which bom of us are living each moment.

The other envelope had your letter.

As I read, my eyes welled up with tears and at the mention of 'ten years', the drops fell.

For ten years my colours and me, and this table drawer shall keep our doors open and wait for you.

This letter of yours is a decision of your pain and I accept it the way I accepted your love.

This ten years' torturous wait, is beckoning me for a union at its end.

Khudda Hafiz (God be with you).

2nd January, 1961

from imroz

49

This long curse of ten years seems almost like a blessing.

The pall of darkness before me is lifted.

I can see a bright ribbon of light, shining over the wall of ten years long wait.

My thoughts have found their direction and destination.

If this is the passion, the warmth and the trust, then not just this decade but many more decades can be sacrificed.

2nd January, 1961 night Jeeti

from imroz

18

I was with you in a garden.

Lying under a tree of yellow flowers and a red purse under my head.

The decade was passing slowly and I heard a shrill noise.

I woke up with a startle.

There was someone at the door.

It was a telegram, your telegram.

When I read your name I felt that the slow and torturous journey of this decade has finished and I am with you.

You are waking me up saying that your night has finished.

At times I keep on staring at that spot on my shoulder where your passionate kisses would leave marks.

I can't see that mark externally.

But I find it deep inside me....

Where I try to find my Aashi.

That Jeeti is just waiting for you now.

Ashamed of himself, drenched in Aashi's colour.

4.00 A.M.

Another day, another time, another letter

Aashi!

I had a talk with the Times group again yesterday – the salary has to be decided. I am asking for fifteen hundred and they are ready for twelve hundred.

But they like my work a lot.

Yesterday they took me around to their printing department. Their machine can print 20,000 copies in an hour, complete with stitching etc.

But I am not happy without you. Had you been here with me, you would have filled the whole house with your innocent delight. Whenever my talent is appreciated I seek your pride-filled eyes around. And thus seeking, I feel lost myself.

Whenever I see something beautiful, a beautiful child, anything beautiful, a pain rises within me – and darkness seems to envelope my being.

I get furious at this pain and at this darkness too and at that time I feel I should forget everything. I should forget you also, but I end up thinking of you all the more.

Why do we lose everything Aashi! And then understand and realise its value. Why? The realisation of my love dawned on me, after I lost it.

Aashi! Is this destiny?

Don't throw me in this darkness for a decade — there is darkness in front of my eyes, my hands, in front of everything, who knows life may come to an end within this decade!

I have understood and I have realised after losing everything. Now understanding, recognition, realisation everything has come, why don't you also come!

11th January, 1961 Waiting for all that I value! Jeeti

from imroz

51

Amrita was not happy with Imroz when she went to Russia, for the first time on 23rd of April, 1961. Imroz gave Jasmine flowers to her when she was leaving for Russia. She just wrote one letter from there. Probably she remembered that she was annoyed and never wrote another one.

The following letter is the only letter Imroz received.

Jeeti!

I am thankful to life for all the beautiful moments it has given me.

I never cared for the price we have had to pay, for a few precious moments of love. I have gone through intense pangs of separation. Despite that I feel the price is not enough.

The moments of our love are far more precious.

This is an alien land and its inhabitants are strangers but they have won my heart with their warmth. I was welcomed with flowers wherever I went. The writers union published an article before I arrived. The tittle, "Welcome to our friend Amrita!"

And yes! Zulfia's hospitality is full of warmth and love. During our interaction, I mentioned, "I have seen the hospitality of life.... but today life in reality seems to have compensated me".

The flowers that you gave me adorned my hair and while saying all this I could feel the fragrance seeping into my being.

25th April, 1961 Tashkend

from imroz

52

My love,

The world is full of deceptions and dreams that are frivolous and short lived.

In you I have found perennial love that is not there anywhere else in the world.

But you don't believe me anymore.

I wish you could recognise my inner being.

I adore you, my incomparable love!

Every moment I visualise being with you and then nothing else matters.

Where are you, love?

15th January, 1961

from imroz

53

My love,

You must have written something new. Why have you not sent it to me?

I am waiting.

My life has come to a standstill – my work, my health, my income, my thoughts, my age — everything has come to a standstill — poised and waiting for someone.

I did not know that one could think about someone like this - I pine for you.

I feel I am meant for you – only for you.

But no one realises the truth without living, without actually experiencing it.

Why do we realise this after losing everything?

But one cannot live just with a realisation. If this realisation is powerless to get me back all what I have lost, then it is of no use.

18th January, 1961 Jeeti

from imroz

54

My love,

This city, this world is full of beauty, full of youth.

There is no dearth of work either and that too for an artist and a worker like me.

But I am not attracted towards anything beautiful nor do I feel like working.

I am just wandering aimlessly.

Aashi! I have recognised my instincts and impulses. The maturity that you always wanted has come now – after so much of suffering.

When conflicts resolved, maturity dawned for me to understand my inner self.

I realised your value, after you left.

Don' be silent like this please.

Now I would never do anything that you dislike. Anything that might hurt you.

I have always told you everything about myself (I tell you all my conflicts).

I hope you understand me.

No one else understands me except you.

I do not care if anyone else does, but you must understand.

My Aashi.

You must understand your own Jeeti.

24th January, 1961

from imroz

55

Aashi!

I did not know that you and you alone are my strongest attraction.

I admit my guilt.

Would you never take this punishment back?

For how long.....

For how long will you save yourself from this torture of separation? Would it be......till my voice is silenced?

27th January, 1961

from imroz

56

Dear Aashi,

I had a home once, but I lost it.

Only a feeling lingers when my being gets seized with your thoughts.

We had woven many dreams together and we were confident that we shall fulfill them all.

Dreams are shattered... but... self-belief lingers.

Are we just dreamers? Can't we pick up the threads of reality? No I don't agree.

If I can dream, I can visualise reality as well. I am not a dream. I am a reality, a solid, and an inevitable reality and so are you...the destiny of all realities.

Look how annoyed I am at my incomplete self.

This annoyance becomes a challenge for a man and then everything in him awakens.

Time always waits...

We shall definitely meet...

27th January, 1961

from imroz

57

Aashi,

I recall a scene from a movie....

...with the help of a rope, a blind girl reaches her bed. One end of the rope is tied to her bed and the other to the door of the bathroom.

I am also walking along the invisible rope of your attraction. One end of this rope is tied to love, to 5th Dec 1960, and the other to the other end of the journey in the darkness of ten years, to 5th Dec. 1970.

The excitement of meeting you has spread a kind of light inside me and I am oblivious of all darkness, as if this darkness of a decade is not actually a decade but a path, a road – a straight road to our house where I see you standing in the doorway, looking towards this road, and I am walking towards you...

... Jeeti who belongs to Aashi.

4th February, 1961

Imroz continued

I have just come back from the station after seeing off Avtaar. Got your letter, my eyes are downcast and my head bent.

The man in me bows.

My pride shattered.

Everything inside me is shattered.

I am in tears.

Radier than writhing in guilt, I feel, this man should bend forever and perish.

I am your pain.

My own darkness.

Jeeti

My queen friend!

Did you go to America to write this novel?

It seems I am reading the book of my own destiny.

My destiny has not been written by God.

But by a poetess.

Only you can do that.

Your Jeeti

The distance of nine hundred miles has vanished. But there is still some distance left, that cannot be seen. This will always remain. Because it is the source of an endless attraction.

Jeeti

from imroz

58

Amrita remained annoyed with Imroz for nearly three years - November 1960 to December 1963. But they met often.

Amrita started building her house in Hauz Khas in 1961.

Together they watched the house being built.

In March, 1962, she started living in the new house.

On the 8th of January, 1964, they started living together.

The following letter conveys the anguish and loneliness of Amrita.

Jeeti!

My life is a long and lonely road.

Misfortunes have waited for me at every turn.

When you were around, there was no place we could call a home.

And now that I have made a nest, you are not there.

Between us there is distance of just a few miles but the lack of social legitimacy makes it look like a distance of another world!

I am restless in a very strange way. I feel this restlessness will outlive my life. Are the two synonyms?

29th March, 1962 Aashi

from imroz

59

Rajinder Singh Bedi, while making his film 'Rano', called Amrita from Bombay and asked her to write a song for his film.

He committed to pay rupees five hundred for the song.

She listened to the music of the song on telephone.

Amrita wrote the song and sent it by post and even dictated it on the telephone.

Whether the song was recorded or not, Amrita did not come to know.

Weeks passed and then months, there was no intimation, no letter or phone call.

After getting the song, Bedi Sahib was quiet and so was his promise.

Once Imroz went to Bombay. Sitting with Sukhbir, the conversation veered around to Bedi Sahib and he asked Sukhbir, "One can hear Bedi Sahib talking, but has anyone ever heard the silent Bedi Sahib? The king of eloquence is really silent these days."

Although Amrita never reminded him of his promise but in the following letter she is referring to this incident.

I don't know why and how, time seems to have come to a standstill.

It is ten in the morning and your letter is about to arrive.

That is when my day shall begin.

Avtar is here these days. Last night Avar, Shelley, Kandla and I saw the film, 'My fair lady'.

I so much wished, I could see this film with you.

Even if your film is never made or your paintings never exhibited, or your hidden talent and beauty never reach the screen or the canvas to come in front of the people, I shall always salute the beauty of your inner being.

My one and only friend!

No one has understood me except you. This is not a complaint that others have not understood me but a great sense of fulfillment that you have.

Just now Avtar was talking what Bedi Sahib said – that Amrita loves money and weighs everything in monetary terms.

I know you would also laugh at this.

Why are people so deceptive, Jeeti!

I never realised that even Bedi was one of them. I thought he had a deep understanding of the human heart, his values were different and he had a penetrating vision.

But everything is superficial.

Few realise how sweet is the morsel, one earns with hard work

People believe in charity and in undeserved rewards. These are nothing but another form of 'loot'.

But few realise how beautiful and satisfying it is to earn one's bread. Accepting the price of one's hard work and giving the rightful due are two sides of the same coin. But some people have one sided beliefs. They feel it is fine to use the hard work that someone has done and not pay them their due. I have deliberately not used the word "give". It carries the stench of charity but getting one's 'due' has a sweet fragrance.

Your hands are full of this fragrance. Love.

Your Maja.

27th April, 1965

from imroz

60

The letters that Amrita wrote in 1966 from Bulgaria and Moscow.

Jeeti!

Coming away from home and from all the familiar faces has led to a strange sense of loneliness!

Looking at the sky at night one sees clouds and just now looking down from the window of the aircraft, I can see clouds again - as if the sky is torn into two and one piece is spread below and the other on top of the body and the mind as well.

There are still two hours to reach Moscow but I just don't know how many hours will the mind take to reach anywhere from this loneliness.

24th May, 1966, 2p.m.

My watch is still having the Indian time. It is 4'O clock.

I have reached Moscow and it is 1.35 in the afternoon here. Checking of the passport, the luggage, the ticket, collecting dinner coupons, has taken one hour.

Had a rather interesting experience. It made me realise how different it is when one is in a state of quest and when one is just a passer-by.

An hour at the airport made me tired. I decided to use a coupon at the restaurant of the airport (just have three in all).

Each coupon can buy things worth one rouble and twenty Copecks. The price of a beer and an egg is almost the same.

The hotel room is good enough to spend the night but there is no arrangement for food. We have to go to the restaurant of the airport for meals. It is four thirty here.

If Darshan comes I will give him this letter to post.

It is 9 at night here and the sun is still bright. It is difficult to adjust to this change. I have been looking at the sun and then at my watch again and again.

I am having coffee with Darshan at the restaurant of the airport and writing to you.

24th May, 1966

from imroz

61

My friend,

Long journeys should either be taken in one's youth or with a companion.

Otherwise journeys tend to give a strong sense of loneliness.

I am writing this letter from my room in hotel Sophia. The hotel is new and is really nice but there is no food arrangement. We have to go to some other hotel for food. Had some tea in the morning in the aircraft but could not get even a cup the whole day.

In the evening I enquired from many places but did not get tea anywhere.

People do not drink tea here.

I am missing the tea Kandla makes for me.

25th May, 1966

from imroz

62

A hot cup of tea, was the first thought in the morning.

I almost called Kandla to say, "Bhopi! A cup of tea, please!"

Finally, found a cup at 8.30 at a nearby hotel.

Here they make weak, insipid tea, with tea bags. Just put a bag in a tea cup and pour hot water. Whatever colour gets filtered through the paper is the colour of the tea.

It is so tasteless!

O, how I long for the tea that sets passions on fire.

I am missing the tea we have back home – it virtually opens the pores of the mind and the body.

When you get this letter, have several cups of tea on my behalf.

26th May, 1966

from imroz

59

Jeeti!

My Sweetheart!

This is the most beautiful place in Sophia. The city is a lush green valley surrounded by high hills that look like frills on all four sides. At certain places, the snow shines like bright silver ribbons.

I am now in a restaurant on the Vitosha hill. It is half an hour's drive from Sophia. The buses reach in 45 minutes.

There is a new surprise at every corner of a road in the hills. The sound of waterfalls and springs splend music in the air. When the water embraces the stones with all its heart and soul, it appears as if the stones are singing. I am thinking if the remaining days of my life are spent living somewhere in the womb of such a hill along with you, I would not just live that life but I would celebrate each moment and savour each drop of life's nectar.

I am missing you so much today, how I wish you were here with me at all these places. I visualised a cottage of wood and stones as your studio here.

A day before I saw a hostel for foreign resident students and thought of Shelley and Kandla.

It is a beautiful place with sprawling lawns.

Some Bulgarian boys and girls are sitting on a big table in this hill restaurant. One of them is playing on a flute, some are singing and others are dancing too.

Yesterday, some musicians from Delhi left for home. I have sent a letter with them. They would post this letter in Delhi. It will reach you faster.

They would also give you a call.

Love to my Shelley and Kandla.

Sophia 30th May, 1966 Your Maja

This letter is for Navraj

Naju!

Scooters are very common here and the price varies between four to five hundred Levas.

The restaurants of Varna are new experiments in architecture — just glass and stones have been used. There is so much for you to do in life after you finish your studies in India.

The world has so much to offer to those who are young and intelligent.

There is also a passion for everything antique.

In Varna there is a 'jungle grove'. Tables and chairs have been made out of tree trunks. There are ladders along the sides of trees and lounges have been made on tree tops. There are ropes and pulleys on one side. The whole structure appears to have been built virtually in air.

People hang the ropes down and pull bowls of wine up from the bar below.

In the bar there are no chairs but just a few swings. People sit in these swings and keep sipping wine from the bowls.

Your Mama

from imroz

64

My Imroz!

Lovers are there in every part of the world.

But Moscow is a city of passionate lovers. They are surely a class apart.

Russia has been home to some of the greatest writers, I should say, lovers of the written word. Gorky, Chekhov, Tolstoy, Pushkin, and so many others, all belong to this country. One has heard of lovers of humanity, and lovers of freedom but people in this country love writers – one can see it from the way they have treasured relics and reminders of the great writers, they certainly deserve to be called great lovers.

Streets and roads are named after these writers, their statues adorn the squares and valuable portraits have been made. The manuscripts written by them, the clothes they wore, the things they touched – knife, spectacles, comb, a letter or may be just a tea-pot – is reverentially kissed by the people.

It is so overwhelming.

The expression of contentment on the faces of people tells clearly that it is a rich nation. However, a visit to these museums shows that the people are rich at heart too!

I am looking at some rare pictures of Gorky in a museum. In his lifetime, Gorky had earned a special friendship and respect from

Lenin. There is a picture of his childhood home as well – a place that is associated with his grandfather's love, abject poverty, beatings and torture.

There are several traces of the mishaps and misfortunes that he went through in this period. There is a picture of the first table on which he wrote his first story, the newspaper that published his story for the first time.

The picture of the Czar's men in front of his house, standing guard in 1902, the wallet with a bullet hole that saved his life when in 1903 the Czar's men fired at him.

The picture of that bloody Sunday – 9th of January 1905 when the Czar ordered fire on the workers protesting peacefully - an act that filled Gorky with so much pain that he wrote an article about the agony and misery of the working class. When this article was published, Gorky was put behind bars by the Czar.

Gorky – prisoner No. 689-9 – and I am in front of the picture of that iron bed from where Gorky wrote such rich literature.

Only a nation of passionate lovers can make such museums and dedicate them exclusively to writers.

18th June, 1966

Amrita

from imroz

65

The letters that Amrita wrote in 1967 from Yugoslavia, Hungary, Romania, Germany and Teheran follow.

Dear Jeeti!

Coming to Europe has been a new experience this time – rather a strange one.

Reached Dubrovnik at six in the evening yesterday.

It should be ten thirty at night in India.

It took half an hour to complete the formalities at the airport and another one to reach the hotel.

I was exhausted and just wanted to sleep.

In the morning I ordered some tea from the restaurant. The hotel is on a beach.

It is a pleasure to sit in the balcony and have my tea.

At nine thirty a girl came and escorted me to the office of the hotel manager, where I realised that they are giving us just the accommodation and the meals are not inclusive.

We could spend seven thousand dinars on food, an amount not sufficient enough to have food at a decent place. They suggested that I could have meals at one of the cheap hotels in the market which is at quite a distance from the hotel.

A bottle of beer costs three hundred dinars and so does a packet of cigarettes. A packet of American cigarettes costs as much as 850 dinars....

Do not have the energy to go out again now, it is so hot. A guide will come to take us for sight-seeing in the evening, I think I shall eat something on the way.

Plays are staged every evening here. It is a beautiful place and attracts many tourists. They lounge at the beaches in their bathing suits.

But it is so lonely. I am alone the whole day.

There is an official arrangement that someone will escort me to the play in the evenings.

People do not understand English here.

Going to the market twice or thrice in a day, to purchase eatables feels very strange and adds to my sense of isolation.

It is six in the evening and I am hungry.

There isn't any restaurant that is open at this rime. They open after seven. Bought a glass of beer and a sandwich from a café for 370 dinars – had the beer but the sandwich was so hard I could not eat it.

I fondly remember the *bhindi sabzi* and stuffed *paneer roti* that Kandla makes.

Excelsior Hotel, 10th August, 1967 Amrita

from imroz

66

My Jeeti,

I was talking to you in my sleep and woke up suddenly.

So let me continue the conversation.

Jeeti, I have had a strange experience this time. In a way it was good.

Being alone in a strange city I could observe people closely. In the market, vendors literally catch your hand and urge you to buy stuff.

Yesterday, a woman was selling red embroidered 'jholas'. She was a bit too persistent. It was an extremely ordinary jhola, I did not buy, but asked the price. The price was 6000 dinars.

Some artists sit reclining against the thick city wall and show their work No one buys these paintings. The life of an artist is full of struggle everywhere.

I keep thinking of you.

The common people earn about two thousand dinars a day which is not enough for decent meals. In the evening I had an omelet and a slice for one thousand and one hundred dinars!

How I wish you were here with me!

We would have been so happy watching the sea-waves quietly. Often, from the balcony, I stare at the huge sails of the ships and then come back to read Henry Miller. Perhaps it is the death instinct in me.

(The life instincts are converted into death instincts).

There is a lingering feeling in my heart — that life has actually gone by. If there remain just a few days more, why should these be lived without you?

Till now I always felt loneliness as something effervescent, something flowing – like tears or maybe like sweat – that can be wiped off easily. But now it feels like a reality, an ugly one – like a carbuncle on the body that can actually be felt and we have to carry its weight around.

11th August, 1967 Maja

from imroz

67

Jeeti!

This time I have written rather sad letters to you.

The moment I see the telephone, I feel like calling you up. This is obsessive madness.

I should try and come out of it.

I have just come back after watching some folk dances. Good performance but I kept thinking of you and Kandla too!

12th August, 1967; 11 o'clock at night.

Your love is a like a lighthouse amid the fathomless waters of loneliness.

In fact, it is both – a lighthouse and a life boat.

At the moment, you, the ocean and Henry Miller are with me. I am reading Henry Miller as if I am going to get a Ph.D. on him.

It is raining heavily today. It appears as if the sea and the sky have mingled into each other.

13th August, 1967 early morning

The control that you have over me, is not normal.

But, what is 'normality'?

In the words of Henry Miller: "Normality is the paradise of escapologists, for it is a fixation concept, pure and simple. It is better, if we can, stand alone and feel quite normal about our abnormality, doing nothing whatever about it, except what needs to be done in order to be oneself".

I cannot do anything about this abnormality. It is a part of my being. It is me.

13th noon

I am not able to meet any writer here.

No one knows English.

13th evening

It seems I have come here this time just to write letters to you.

Feel like talking to you all the time.

Conversation with everyone else comes to a stop but with you it goes on, it moves – just like one breath follows another....

14th August, 1967, early morning *Maja*

Jeeti!

When the limits of reality overwhelm, we seek refuge in fantasy.

But I think if we find something with patience, it is even beyond that. That is where you stand for me - beyond fantasy.

In the words of Henry Miller, all art shall finish one day. But artists will not. And life will not be "an art" but just "art".

If we agree that the time of Henry Millers vision will come in about a thousand years then I would like to say that you are born a thousand years earlier.

It is your fault.

It is a mistake committed by all those who live life completely with all their heart and soul.

People do not have the courage to live like this – they lead a fragmented life – perhaps some part of them dies within the womb even before they are born.

The sight of a complete man is agonising for such people.

So the neglect that this world has meted out to you is rather natural.

Each present moment has its roots in the past.

But what can one say about a person like you whose present has its roots in the future.

If today I am able to buy a newspaper that will be published after thousand years, I am confident that I would be able to read the praise of your talent and creative powers that have otherwise remained locked up in your room.

I cannot associate the word "perfection" with you. It reflects something stagnant, still and cold – something to which nothing can be added or deducted. You are more akin to "progress", leaving something behind each day and finding something new everyday.

The word "perfection" is like the portrait of Jesus Christ that adorns the walls of a church and when you stand in front of this picture, everything comes to a standstill.

Talking to you gives the feeling of being alive. It is like a continuity, just like breathing. Are you not Christ come alive!

Writing to you from an alien country has reminded me that today is the fifteenth of August. The day our country got Independence.

If a human being can symbolise a day, I would like to say that you are my fifteenth of August.

The day I came to you.

My existence, my being was liberated.

Dubrornik Amrita

from imroz

68

Whenever Amrita went abroad or Imroz went to Bombay in search of livelihood, letters were their mainstay.

The following letters were written during the days Amrita was in Yugoslavia.

Dear Aashi,

Manoj* rang up this morning.

I went to meet him in his hotel. In the course of the conversation, he talked about making a Punjabi movie.

Something solid like Punjab and truthful like Punjabis.

The conversation veered around to your novel 'Pinjar'. Manoj has read this novel.

I narrated the story again in my own words - the frame and development of characters, the surroundings and the Punjabi culture that permeates the surrounding.

Manoj listened with great sensitivity and kept asking questions. It appears something might come out of it.

It was time for Bhopi*1 to come home, so I came back

---

* Film actor and producer Manoj Kumar

*1 Amrita's daughter Kandla

And I started talking to you, sometimes sitting in my room or standing in yours.

I saw Puro*2, sitting on an empty jute bag, shelling peas and Rashida on horseback.

There were so many voices calling out Waris Shah....

19th August, 1967 Jeeti

*2 Puro and Rashida, characters from Amrita's novel 'Pinjar'

from imroz

69

It is 21st today and my last day in this city of Dubrovnik.

Tomorrow at nine in the morning, I have to leave for Okhrid and from there to Struga, where an evening of poetry will be held and from there back to Belgrade.

My books weigh so much and I have come to know that cost of excessive baggage will not be paid by the organisers. If I have to pay that fare in the morning, I will not have any money left for food. We have already been paid for 21 days.

...

Today on 22nd, I have reached Okhrid.

Last evening I bought a net bag and put all my books in that and the rest in a big handbag.

My arms are aching with the weight of these bags, but fortunately I didn't have to pay, for excessive baggage.

These people do not even offer a glass of water in the aircraft here. It was such a long journey, I am almost half-dead. Thank God the journey is over for the time being at least!

Okhrid is situated by the side of a big lake. Poets from different countries have come. It would be a gathering of nearly two hundred and fifty poets. For three consecutive days, that is, 25th, 26th and 27th, poetry evenings will be held.

Just after my arrival I noticed that they have translated my poem *'Aag di baat'* into English.

My arms are aching and I am tired after lifting so many books but I think it has all been worth it.

Everyone is delighted with 'Naagmani' and are rather surprised that such literary magazines are published in India.

They seem to be resenting that there is no publication like this in their language.

Your Maja

from imroz

70

Jeeti love!

I read a poem in the assembly at Struga today.

The response was so overwhelming that it moved me to tears. I did not know that people loved writers so much.

I have not been appreciated back home in Punjab and I am rather used to being neglected. The feeling of being loved and recognised is new to me and ironically it has come from aliens.

I am sending an article for 'Naagmani' You can use it for the new edition. I had written an article while I was in Dubrovnik but that one is twenty pages long and I have not been able to copy it. I will publish it in the December issue of 'Naagmani' after my return.

There is an invitation from Germany to come there for a week. I shall confirm the date when I reach Belgrade.

There is an invitation from Tehran also, for three days, through our embassy. But the journey would be a bit too long and tiring!

28th August, 1967 Maja

from imroz
71

Maja!

Just leave all the domestic burdens and responsibilities on us for these three months.

These three months Amrita should spend with Amrita, the writer.

Bhopi is the same sweet and loving.

Her mama has been included in her uncle.

This sense of addition and inclusion is a new feeling, rather a first experience.

I work the whole day like Jeeti and stay at home the whole day like you, for the house and for both our daughters*3.

My every letter would be a toast to you.

23rd August, 1967 Jeeti

3 Kandla and Naagmani

from imroz

71

The letter that Imroz wrote to Amrita on her birthday, when she was in Hungary.

My dear Aashi,

The day, today is full to the brim.

The day is filled with all the seasons of the year, the colours of all seasons and their fragrance.

It seems filled with all the festivals.

With all poetry and purity.

With the bright suns of all 365 days; I am raising a toast to 'today' – to the 31st of August and to your existence, along with all the suns of half a century and to all the suns of the coming century.

31st August, 1967 Jeeti

from imroz

73

My Dear!

Reached Belgrade early yesterday morning and received three letters from you.

It felt as if you were there at the airport to receive me.

And now as I am writing to you, I feel I am celebrating my birthday.

I visited the bohemian street last night.

Poets, actors and painters get together here for a month in keeping with a tradition that began in the nineteenth century.

At night they light candles on the walls to see paintings, stage old plays and see silent movies of the nineteenth century.

Someone is frying fish on one side.

They read poems and eat kababs. Last night they had called me; heard my poems and served kababs.

An actor rendered the translation of my poems so beautifully that I would always remember this evening.

31st August, 1967 Your Maja

from imroz

74

My love Jeeti!

I reached Hungary at one in the afternoon.

After the glamour of Belgrade, the old buildings of Hungary appear sad and silent.

Dust of long years seems to have sattled on them.

But yesterday evening there was a meeting of P.E.N. writers at five. I met many writers there. Mr. Hubah, who had come to meet us in Delhi at our place, was also there along with many other poets. The warmth was all around.

In Belgrade, unexpectedly Jambery, a poet from East Africa, brought flowers for my birthday. He had read about my birthday, in 'The Black Rose'.

See, how the written word spreads its shoots.

That day I shopped till the afternoon. For you I bought a transistor and a shirt with Yugoslavia's national embroidery. Some records for Shelley, jeans and a top for Kandla also with national embroidery.

Prices are strange and unreasonable here.

Transistors are very cheap – cheaper than shirts.

I went to a town, at a distance of a hundred and twenty five miles from Belgrade, where in 1941, the German army slaughtered every single person – seven thousand – in a single day.

The poem 'A tale of blood', (*Khoon di katha*) that was published in Naagmani was written on this tragic incident.

It is about the children of this city.

There are two pillars erected in the memory of the dead, symbolising the mauled and mutilated life of these children.

The pillars are about eighteen yards broad and stand ten yards tall. Innocent faces of the children are engraved on the stones.

Some of their notebooks with their names and some geometry equations have been kept in the museum.

Dragi - seventh standard...

Shilia - sixth standard..........

Also, there are two statues of white marble.

One of a man and another of a woman, symbolising seven thousand dead people!

Beautiful and exquisite pieces of sculpture.

I have never seen pain engraved in stones earlier.

The Yugoslavian sculpture is rather advanced.

Before leaving the town, I visited the Belgrade museum yesterday. As exhibition of the paintings of Picasso was going on. An exhibition of Mexican art was also there, saw that too.

This art presents a strange amalgamation of human and animal shapes.

Remembered you wherever I went. We should have seen all this together.

A Yugoslavian woman, who lived in a German concentration camp, is still alive. I could not meet her for lack of time but saw the statues made by her and a self-portrait in iron and stone – a picture of pain in iron.

The people of Yugoslavia - the city where seven thousand people were slaughtered, is calling me again on 21st of October for a week. They want that I should recite the poem we published in Naagmani – the translation of *'Khoon di katha'*.

But it is very difficult to go again.

Anyway, I shall see.

Maja

75

from imroz

O my dear!

The letter that you wrote on the 31st arrived yesterday.

If one life is not sufficient to get such a letter, it is reason enough to be born again.

You are my 31st August and all the three sixty five days of the year as well.

Such a letter has the potency to produce a future – even from a barren present like this.

I have received the new edition of Naagmani in Hungary. It is for the first time that I have felt each page of Naagmani like a reader living far away.

The tide is really beautiful, but there are many mistakes left uncorrected in the proofs.

I had sent an article from Okhrid about the poetry evening in Satruga, please keep it carefully. It is not to be published yet. I had written an article in Belgrade also, we shall publish everything together in one edition along with the pictures.

From here I will go to Romania on the 22nd, and then to Sophia on the 12th of the next month and on 20th to Germany.

Tomorrow on the 8th we shall go on the bank of a lake for four days. There is a rest house there.

Hungary appears sad and dusty at first sight but it unveils its beauty gradually.

At night, the city of Budapest on the banks of the river Danube looks beautiful with all its shinning lights.

Mr. Mishra, who along with Mr. Nathan, had translated Hindi poems into English, is also here in the same hotel. He will be going to America for two years.

He has brought Ganga jal along with him.

Yesterday I recited to him a line from my poem - from Gangajal to Vodka, the journey of my parched lips.

7th September, 1967 Your Maja

from imroz

71

My Poetess!

You do not belong to one earth, one nation, one language or one community.

You belong to every such place where the earth is vast like the heart and is fragrant with emotions.

You belong to every such nation where poetry and artists can progress and are free of all restrictions.

You belong to every such language that has the power to touch the heart.

You belong to every such community whose people do not live in the days gone by. Who live in the pure and sacred present moment and like the present they are alive to their own self and know how to live with others.

And, you belong to every such night and every such day where each night conceives a new creation in its womb. Each morning rises, humming a new song.

Maja, you must go to Romania and to West Germany also. People are calling you and waiting for you with so much of love and affection.

You are restless without me and I am impatient without you. In the guise of this restlessness, I would be with you everywhere, in every country, in every city, in every gathering.

I would be present wherever you go.

In the languages of all these nations, I would manifest in new ways, having some other names which you may find difficult to pronounce but you would always recognise me easily.

In every new building you would discover something new of mine and you shall see my bearing.

From every old Church you will recognise my footsteps.

You shall see my colour in each flower.

Inhale my fragrance from the breeze.

You will know my depth from every lake.

Recognize me in the flow of every river.

I shall gaze upon your face again and again from every new thought of a poem and from the pulsating rhythm of every song.

Maja!

I will never let you get tired.

Every morning I will awaken in your eyes like new enthusiasm and I shall fill your footsteps with a refreshing energy to cover the journey of life.

My Poetess!

You must go to Tehran, the house of rich Persian poetry – it is a nation alive and fragrant with the spirit of Omar Khayam and his rubbaiyat.

My Aashi,

When you would be thinking of Omar Khayam standing under

some Persian arch, I would be watching the mingling of another rubai in the rubbaiyat of Omar Khayam.

O my Akhrid lake, do you know that here, an ocean is waiting for you.

2nd September, 1967 *Jeeti*

from imroz

77

Maja!

The wait for your letters makes me feel like a musical instrument.

The day dawns and touches my strings and gives way to the night.

But at night – no song awakens, nothing comes alive.

Since the past 30 days, I am living in this torture - the torture of silence.

I am living this torture in the shape of a day whose life is stagnant.

O my sun! When shall you rise from the west?

Do you know that since the past one month – the day has not risen here and there has been just one long dark night?

A night that is three months long.

Just received your letter.

It is like the sun rising from the sky-blue papers of Hungary.

9th September, 1967 Jeeti

from imroz

78

Maja!

A sun rises in the sky - the common sun, common and shared by the entire earth. Everything on this earth lights up with the light of this sun. Everything lives with its warmth and gets nurtured.

A sun rises on the earth too, a special one for the world of the heart.

In fact, it rises just for one heart. It transforms a thought into a bond and changes a dream into a reality.

This sun rises in the shape of a human being and it has many facets just like a human being.

Generally, this sun is meant for one individual only but often it becomes a shared one, like the sun of the skies. However, when it rises as an incarnation of a god, a guru or a saint, it becomes the sun that that shines for everyone.

I saw this sun for the first time in the guise of a writer, a poetess. It may be destiny or just a stroke of good luck

I discovered it.

Made it mine in the shape of a woman.

A friend.

An artist and a beloved.

13th September, 1967 Jeeti

from imroz

79

Yesterday, the Indian ambassador sent somebody to greet me at the airport and invite me to his place.

At the moment my room is full of bright crimson flowers from two countries. A farewell bouquet from Yugoslavia and a welcome one from Hungary.

I have got an invitation from Romania. I would stay there till the fifteenth of October and then go to Bulgaria and Germany.

On the way back I would stop in Tehran for three days. I would be back home, in the first week of November.

One does not get good tea in Hungary, but coffee is good. The tea is almost bitter and feels sticky.

In the morning the Indian Embassy sent me a big packet of Indian tea.

Fascism is an ugly reality.

Honestly Jeeti, one cannot realise this fact in India. Europe has lived this experience. The smoke left on the walls of many cities in Hungary bear the imprint of bombs. They look peeled and black

A few monuments of the dead and some pictures are just what are left.

Give my love to Candy and Naagi.

Your Maja

from imroz

80

My Jeeti!

Your letters have so much power on me.

They gently suggest that I should continue my work here and their warmth beckons me back home.

Has Shelly ever written from Baroda or not? Kandla is always there in my thoughts.

My interpreter has just arrived.

She has brought your letter from the office.

Jeeti my life!

Each letter of yours comes like a breath of fresh air.

16th September, 1967 Your Maja

from imroz
81

My dear artist - the creator of my Naagi.

The Hungarian writers are very gentle and perceptive. Simple at heart, sensitive and pure in intentions. They have a quest for knowledge and a thirst for the literature of the world.

Naagmani has been profoundly appreciated by them. We meet often and every time they come, they bring flowers for me. My room remains fragrant with fresh flowers everyday.

Presendy, Penguin is publishing books of two Hungarian poets. These writers seem keen to experiment. For nearly a decade their writing was under a strict surveillance.

Their real voice was suppressed.

But now an acceptance has come. One of them came to listen to the poems of Gysenberg which I recited. He was almost ecstatic and wondered why such poems were still not published in his country.

Today, when I am about to leave Hungary, I have received three of your letters. The ones that you wrote on the 6th, the 12th, and the 13th.

I feel as if both of us are going to Romania together.

22nd September, 1967 Your Maja

from imroz
82

It is amazing, my sweetheart Jeeti!

As I reached Romania at 10.15 p.m., there was a message that I should visit the embassy sometime during the day.

After having tea, I went and found that two of your letters were waiting for me.

I felt as if you had reached Romania before me. It seemed, you were here to receive me with all your warmth.

Your existence has the power to obliterate all distances. It imbibes both the journey and the destination. It is constant like reality and all-pervasive like the flight of fancy.

If I like something in this world it is because you are there and we share the same earth and the same sky.

After collecting your letters, I went sight-seeing in the city with my interpreter.

The balconies of all the buildings of the city - even the tall ones - are full of flowers.

Statues adorn the crossings and the road dividers look beautiful with flowers weaving red and green patterns on them.

It is a very pleasant city. There are many gardens and lakes here.

There was an invitation from the writers union.

Do you remember Zaharia Stancu? I once mentioned him in one of my articles in the context of his novel, 'Barefoot.' Later I met him in Delhi at the Asian Writer's Conference.

He is the president of the union here. Today we were together at lunch. There were some Russian writers also.

The lunch started at two in the afternoon and finished at five in the evening.

There were long and poetic toasts.

One of the toasts of the Russian writers was "the word 'poetry' belongs to the female gender.. .So after meeting Amrita we can say that poetry was born in India".

There were other toasts also.

And mine was... In our language, the word 'Saki' means the one who fills and serves wine. At that time Zaharia was filling wine into our glasses. If 'Saki' is translated into the Romanian language it means Zaharia.

And my life Jeeti!

The biggest toast of my life is to you.

Narad Hotel, Bucarest, 23rd September, 1967 Your Maja

My ticket to Germany has not reached the Indian Embassy.

The spokesperson at the German embassy said that the ticket had been dispatched from there. They sent a cable and found out the ticket number also, but the ticket could not be located. Finally a senior Romanian citizen suggested that we should check at the office of the Airlines. They often keep the tickets and do not deliver them. After much harassment, we came to know that the ticket was actually lying at the office of the Airlines.

Sarcastically, some people said that if they get replies to their letters in sixty days from the offices, they consider themselves lucky.

This is also a facet of socialism.

12th September, 1967 Your Maja

from imroz

83

Maja!

Sitting alone I am thinking that you must have reached West Germany.

Just listen to the calculations of my thoughts.

West Germany plus ten days, plus Amrita, is equal to a beautiful journey.

Bhopi is wearing a saree today. The way she is walking all around the house, it appears a little bird has suddenly got wings.

She is waiting for her boyfriend.

She is pacing around the room restlessly. She stops to drink water. She comes to look outside from the verandah. She goes back to the room to look at her reflection in the mirror, as if she has to look at herself time and again, along with her wings.

So today's calculation is - youth plus dreams, plus waiting is equal to madness.

This is perhaps the last bit of our conversation through letters.

By the time you get this letter, you would be in the middle of your preparations for the journey back home.

Me and my candles shall wait for our Diwali, which I shall

celebrate three days after the common Diwali that falls on the first. And when you come these candles will be lit.

This house will be bright with light.

So also will be my life and all my existence too!

21st October, 1967 Jeeti

from imroz

84

My Artist!

The soul of my pen seems to be on a quest - going to the door step of each and every Punjabi.

It seeks to tell them a sad story.

I am sitting in the B.P.T. library of Romania. It is an abbreviation. It means Everyman's Library.

The owners of this library publish a book every week Each book has around four to five hundred pages. Usually the first edition is of 75,000 copies. Every book runs into several editions - some have even 20.

This weekly publication can be the work of a Romanian writer or a translation. They publish both native and foreign literature. The publishing industry here is indeed very prolific. One book is published every one and a half day.

In 1931, the first edition of a book by a very eminent poet of the country was published with five hundred copies. After fourteen years, someone needed that book and came to know that those five hundred copies were still not sold.

In the year 1963, something suddenly happened, there was a huge demand for this book. The people had suddenly discovered the writer. That year a second edition with 6,000 copies was published and after twenty four hours of the publication, it was difficult to find even a single copy. And then the next edition of 20,000 copies was published followed by another one of 80,000 copies.

Isn't this a dream come true for writers?

All this is beyond comprehension for me. Why do such dreams remain unrealised most of the time?

Every Romanian seems to have a passion for books.

On every 1st of the month they go to a book shop with their salary to buy their favourite books.

The publishers told me that the number of books published this year is much less than the demand. So from next week they would publish two books every week instead of one. Expensive books are also published. These are priced around eighty to hundred lei. The weekly publication is priced at five lei.

How do dreams fall within the limits of comprehension.

May be this is the quest of my writing too.

This is what the soul of my pen wanted to ask people back home.

Sitting here in Romania I can feel the tears flowing from my words.

Upset and disturbed they wander aimlessly in the streets of Punjab.

26th September, 1967 Yours Amrita

from imroz

85

"O Allah! What is there beyond Gaur?"

There is a story that seeing the delicious food being served to Brahmins, a non-Hindu got so tempted that he wanted to join the feast. A friend advised him to wear a dhoti and kurta and sit in the queue with the others. If someone enquired about him he should simply say that he was a Hindu. If they further ask "which Hindu", he should reply that he was a Gaur Hindu.

His style of sitting gave him away and someone asked him who he was. He promptly replied that he was a "Gaur Hindu". The reply could not satisfy the curiosity, so someone asked him "which Gaur." Now he was totally flabbergasted and muttered in confusion, "O Allah! What is there beyond Gaur."

My friend, I told you about the profusion of the Romanian publishing industry yesterday. But I have come to know that publishing a book in a day and a half was just the score of one publishing house. Today I went to Universal Literature Publishing house. In this tiny nation of two million people, 8,000 new books are published every year which means eight million copies and this amounts to four books per person.

Various categories of books are published – poetry, old and contemporary classics, histories of literature, art of drama, research and criticism.

They have also translated a huge bulk of world literature – some from American literature, from Latin America, Soviet Literature, French, English and German literature as well.

From Indian literature there are excerpts from the Mahabharata, Ramayana and the Upanishads as well as the works of Kalidas and Tagore. From contemporary Indian literature, they have published some works of Prem Chand, R. K. Narayanan, Yashpal, Renu, Shivshankar Pillay, Raja Rao and Rajinder Yadav.

Difficult reads and expensive books like 'Shakespearean criticism', 'Humanism in America', 'A history of Latin literature', as well as 'A History of North American Literature', 'A History of Contemporary Literature' are also published.

I just want to say "O Allah".

I am feeling the touch of these books that are bound in leather and silk and it feels I am touching a dream.

My darling Imroz!

I am a little upset – on 21st of October, the German army had slaughtered 7,000 people in a city in Yugoslavia. I have already spent the month of August in Yugoslavia. Desanka Maksimovic has invited me to come again on the 21st.

Desanka Maksimovic, the Yugoslavian poetess, had written a poem in the memory of the 300 dead children. They wanted me to recite the translation of the poem on that day.

I have been visiting so many countries since the past two and a half months. So I postponed this invitation to another year and came to Germany instead of Yugoslavia.

It is a strange coincident that it was the same date when I reached Germany, 21st of October.

I had seen so much of Eastern Europe, but it was for the first time that I had come to the western part. There was a strong restlessness.

On this particular date, I did not go to the place where 300 children were murdered but instead I have come to the country whose army was responsible for the slaughter!

On that date, a writer, Heinrich Boll, was to be given Germany's George Buchner award in Frankfurt. I was also invited for this function but when I went, my heart was not with me.

"You are honouring me for celebrating and interpreting human feelings here but Lam not really happy receiving this honour. A few miles away from here Vietnam is being bombarded and I amhelpless, unable to do anything......"

The world of politics is altogether different from the world of humanity. I know that very well.

Still the first thing that I asked the first German writer whom I met was, "What was the plight of the writers in the days of Hitler?"

"There were three options – death, exile and silence", a German novelist, smiled and said, "not just during that time but even ten years later, there were just these three options – one was to live an absolutely lifeless and listless life, another was to accept everything and try to live on and the third one was to somehow connect oneself with the people and try to analyse the reasons behind the holocaust."

"Karl Marx was born here," Davy said, showing me the pictures of some historical monuments and added, "Even before him, his theory was brought into existence by George Buchner. He died when he was 23. Only if he had been alive..." Looking at Goethe's house in Frankfurt and Schiller's in Stuttgart, I was thinking this land has produced such eminent philosophers but and my interpreter Mrs. Muller smiled and said, "Hitler was an Austrian, not a German" and what Davy had said in Frankfurt echoed in my ears "That time is unforgivable. The people and their literature are still carrying that cross. Our philosopher (Adorno) has said the people of this language have terrorised and tortured millions of innocents."

How can anyone write a story or a poem in that language!

Now I am not restless.

A strange serenity has descended.

And I can say that a language, capable of such thoughts and sensitivity, is capable of great creativity as well.

26th October, 1967 Yours Amrita

from imroz

86

Jeeti,

Yesterday I watched a play by Bretcht.

Have to go to Munich by the evening train.

There is an invitation from Tehran but I am still waiting for the visa. And there is no connecting flight between Rome and Tehran. If I do not go to Tehran, I will come back home earlier.

Dear Imroze!

It is eleven at night.

Tomorrow, at this time, I will reach Tehran. I will get a direct flight to Tehran from Frankfurt. Munich is the biggest cultural centre in the west of Germany.

Hitler was tried in this city. The people here do not even like to utter Hitlers name. If they have to talk about him they just say Mr. H.

The people in the southern part of Germany are unlike their northern counterparts temperamentally. They are strangely simple and warm. They do not think that people of the north are similar to them in any way.

The evening today was filled with German folk songs – from seven in the evening to almost eleven in the night.

I kept eating fruit dipped in Cognac and just enjoyed the song filled evening. One of the songs was

> 'Today in Boavria – aliens have come
> They have come from America
> They have come from France
> From Berlin.'

So people who have come from Berlin are also aliens for them, just like people from America, or from France.

The restaurant where these songs were sung had a specific rustic ambience.

The music comes primarily from the bells around the neck of the cattle.

People drink beer from wooden flasks, eat white sausages and fruit laced with cognac.

They clap and whistle and sing songs as they join the actors. Sometimes the waiters give paper moustaches to them. People stick these moustaches under their nose and dance.

The evening began with simple but serious folk songs.

> There was a tree outside the city wall
> And I wrote many songs under that tree
> And wove many dreams under that tree
> Strong winds have taken the cover away from my head.
> There is no peace, but people say
> Far away there is a tree, and you get peace there.'

I think – whatever is out of reach only that is beautiful.

And slowly the folk songs become lighter in vein.

'Both girls are pretty, one is extremely beautiful
But – I will marry the other one
Her parents have five cows more.'

And then some humour from folk life.

Whatever you may say, there is no comparison with the freedom of speech and the written word of democratic countries. See some samples of their humour:

"Our tram fares have gone up but we do not have to worry. At times our mayor leaves his car and takes a tram ride, just for publicity. Last time he did not buy the ticket. I shall also emulate him and will not buy the ticket."

"Our chancellor could not win the elections this time. Not to worry, he will now go to America and work as Johnson's waiter."

"Our finance minister is very busy these days. What exactly is he doing ? Saving money to give some loan to the Shah of Iran."

"If Russians and Americans meet in space, how will they talk? There will be no interpreter there, very simple – they shall speak German."

"I write my songs with all my heart. I keep adding new ones every day. I am not a slave like the prime minister of our country who writes his speech on a paper and then reads it out. He cannot add a single line to it. But I add many to my songs."

Yesterday afternoon I visited a concentration camp about 20 kilometers away from the town.

One of the most horrifying massacres of history took place here. In this camp, in 1945 on 20* of April, 32,335 Jews were massacred and this is just the figure of a single camp.

Such camps were there at many places.

Even the Germans cannot understand why all this happened. I had gone with a group. The eyes of many German girls were wet with tears.

One of the German girls caught my arm and asked, "Do you think we shall have to pay for the deeds of our people?"

The country is still the same but the thinking has changed. Huge posters have come up all over the city: "Whoever is party to Johnson's Vietnam Policy is one of the murderers."

How should the boundless human energy be used constructively?

History has repeatedly posed this question.

The philosophy of an entire nation looked for an answer and deprived itself of life while another nation tried to explore each layer of life for an answer.

But at the moment all philosophies and opinions are directionless.

The West is looking towards the East and the East is aping the West.

Almost every nation is facing this situation but people are dealing with it according to their level of sensitivity.

There is one thing that I would say about Germany - that even the common man is extremely sharp, alert and aware. My guide is also a beautiful and intelligent girl. While standing beside me she looked intently at the posters about Vietnam and her eyes moistened with sympathy.

At that time I felt that every letter in the poster became dark and engraved deep.

21st October, 1967 Yours Amrita

from imroz

87

Honestly, Imroz!

At times reading one's poem is like feeling one's own pulse.

It is always a particular poem that makes me feel like this. There are many poems which make you feel that you are touching some part of your body, of your being, but there is only one poem that makes me feel that I have put my hand on my pulse.

I cannot say that this is true of all poets, but this is how I felt.

The Punjabis living in Tehran invited me for a few days while I was on my way back from Europe.

They wanted me to recite a few poems. I also wanted to have a feel of those poems all over again and I agreed to their proposal.

One of them had read some of my books, others had just heard my name and invited me.

While reading the poems, I could feel that I was the reader and the listener as well.

But I just went on reading the poems and read those I wanted to listen myself. If I was the listener and the reader both then why not read those that I wanted to listen to.

There were five or six poems but while reading a particular one, I felt that I had put my fingers on my pulse.

This feeling was not sudden. It had been growing inside me for some time.

Yesterday a party was hosted by an Iranian Aamir. Such parties are being hosted in connection with the coronation of the Shah of Iran.

This time the venue was a house where the tradition of music spreads like Iranian carpets.

There was this peculiar ambience of poetry, notes of guitar that can make you tremble and then I met Ani – Qurratulain Hyder.

I like her cold friendship.

It is like chilled whisky and all this led to a strange sense of satisfaction within me, the kind that comes from a sip of wine that lights a fire within and also intoxicates.

Many exotic delicacies were served at the party. One was known as -*Tah-e-degh*. The rice was in a separate dish but its lower portion that stuck to the dish was removed and served separately. That is why it is called *Tah-e-degh*.

The name smiled at me and asked – "if I was to call one of my poems by this name, which one would it be?"

The answer was inherent in the question like the silent echo of the strings of the guitar.

I just had to touch it with a finger tip.

And now let us raise a toast to the poem that is my *Tah-e-degh*.

Today after reading some other poems I read this poem again and did not feel like reading any after that.

It was impossible for me to feel any other poem after that.

If I was to read anything it would have been the same poem again and again.

However I did not want to burden others with my desires, so I did not read anything after that.

Now before going to sleep, I want to read it once again and listen to it on my own.

So I started writing to you.

I am writing the poem too!

Last night
I filled a glass
With the wine of thoughts
The thoughts were crimson
Friends drank them
And raised many toasts
To such words
That are not born in the heart
On which trees do they flower?
And how do they reach the lips?
There was no time to think about this
Or should I say, I was too scared to think
There was a celebration of words.
An anniversary of illusions
I was there
So was the night
And the wine of thoughts
And so many friends.
Friends, who had been invited
And friends who came uninvited
But there was one
Who did not come
Even after so many invitations.

I just said that I wanted to read this poem again and listen to it again just by myself.

This does not mean that it cannot reach you the way it reaches me.

It is just this that, at the moment I do not want it to reach anywhere, not even you.

At the moment I want to keep it to myself, travelling from me to me.

I am writing to you and sending you the poem too – only because this "me", the way I am today, exists and lives for "you".

Earlier this "me" lacked many things, but had plenty of years in the kitty of life. But the "me" that lives today has so much more despite the fart that the years to be lived are few.

All that I have acquired over the years is because of your being there.

I am still keeping the poem just to myself.

But thank you for what you are.

2nd November, 1967 Yours Amrita

from imroz

88

This world appears like a big newspaper to me today, all the words of this newspaper - from the heading to each printed line - are surrounded by a strange sense of nervousness... it is a weird congregation of action and reaction.

If one word talks about achieving new heights, so many others are enveloped in some horrifying darkness.

If one is dreaming of reaching the moon, thousands and millions of others announce that they can destroy millions of dreams with atom bombs.

If one word talks of love and takes the shape of Amrita Pritam and the poetry of love, millions of others spread hatred through books of hatred that they call scriptures.

If I could help it, I would erase all the letters of this newspaper and write just one word, just one – Amrita, who would transform into poetry in no time and then spread all over and become one civilization – from east to west.

6th December, 1967 Jeeti

from imroz

89

Because of work, Imroz had to leave Delhi and go to Bombay several times. It was exile in itself. Imroz felt lonely in Bombay and Amrita remained alone in Delhi. The following letters were written during those days.

Dear Jeeti,

Living here in Delhi, I am a part of your exile – a part of my Jeeti's exile.

Just now I read a line from a Japanese novel. 'Herein lay the loneliness implicit in its vitality'. It appears as if this line is referring just to you.

We have to pay for our vitality with our loneliness. But thankfully, now my loneliness is mingled into yours and yours into mine.

Like a piece of silence broken from silence. A particle of ray separated from light.

It is drizzling today. So I am not able to go to the post office. I will send some money through money order in a day or two.

Last evening two writers from Czechoslovakia came. They were thoroughly impressed by the special issue of 'Naagmani'. When they appreciated the designs of each and every issue, I felt as if with every word they were talking about you.

I am a part of you.

But when people talk of your talent and creative power, I stand at a distance and look at you with reverence.

27th November, 1967 Your Maja

from imroz

90

Aashi,

Sitting with a producer, we were talking of movies, the creative world seems deprived and destitute – starved of good stories.

In this starved state it wandered and then came to Amrita Pritam. From Amrita to 'Dr. Dev', to 'Pinjar', to 'Chk No. 36'.

The producer appears to be intelligent and sensitive. He has called me to make the designs, after reading your novels.

"Who knows"... this phrase envelops all my desires and dreams.

If those dreams are fulfilled, my exile may change into my Ayodhaya - my home, and each moment of my life shall be spent in your benign reign, your 'Ramraj'.

Exile 9th December, 1967 Jeeti

from imroz

91

Aashi,

It was evening and the sun was slowly sinking into the ocean. The air was filled with softly pink mist – as if it was singing the swan song of the day.

When that song finishes, another one is bora out of its ashes and lives – till the next song.

As Babban and I were driving towards the house of Meena Kumari, we were experiencing and looking at all this through the window of the car.

There was this road in Juhu, absolutely quiet and surrounded with the beauty of the fragrant evening.

Meena's house is a cottage on a beach, simple and quiet.

She took us to her room. Babban was discussing some scenes of his film with her. I was looking at the articles in the room. Everything in the room communicated the simple nature of its owner.

Meena has read your novel, 'Pinjar' and she is so impressed.

It is morning now.

I begin my wakeful state with this letter.

This day will finish with a struggle.

This letter connects me to you.

The struggle will help us realise our dream.

Exile 11th December, 1967 Jeeti

92

from imroz

Maja,

Since yesterday this city is breathing with a sense of fear. Even today, people are afraid and terrified.

People are so scared of yesterday's earthquake that they have left their houses and are spending the night in the parks.

Many of the top floors of buildings have been vacated, the place from where this city gets its electric supply has been the worst hit.

The entire town looks distressed.

The cinema halls, studios, factories, mills of the city have been half shut because there is no electricity. This destruction is obvious but what no one can see is the destruction of everything i.e. humane.

The "present" is breathing in a state of fear.

This fear has spread all around in the atmosphere – from every lie to each truth, from infidelity to fidelity, from hunger to luxury, from blankness to art, from war to peace, from destruction to construction, from captivity to freedom.

Generosity and humanitarian feelings are falling apart — piece by piece. It seems the foundations have been eroded and so have the foundations of feelings, of beauty, of the sanctity of words.

Maja!

Is'nt this a tragedy that man is unable to have and possess anything despite the fact that the earth has plenty?

Even after reaching the moon, his search has lost its direction.

Exile 13th December, 1967 Jeeti

from imroz

93

My miracle, My Maja,

May the New Year be a happy one!

Amen!

31.12.67 Jeeti

Aashi,

It is noise all around.

People are screaming in happiness. This noise has enveloped the place like mist, like smoke it has invaded everything and everyone from insignificant huts to sky scrapers alike, from the dusty earth to the moon and the stars, from Quran to the Bible and from the first breath of life to the last.

The poetry of life is scattered and lost in this noise.

Every poem is like a silence hung on the cross of paper.

Each painting appears trapped and colourless on the canvas. Every art is getting buried in the ruins of our limbs.

And I am in the middle of this noise. Away from it and still an inseparable part of it.

And now I am listening to the noise of the beginning of the New Year.

But this voice is not that of congratulations and celebrations. I am unable to feel this celebration.

Deep inside me, there is chasm created by this noise, a chasm between me and celebrations.

1st January, 1968 Jeeti

from imroz

94

Maja!

I am trying to find my way through a dark night.

The direction depends on my footsteps.

In this desolate city I am looking for my dreams.

The sky is desolate too and I am waiting for the sun of imagination to emerge.

The days gone by appear like a shabby cluster of broken huts and I am trying to locate a moment, a moment buried somewhere under these. The present that is, there is my vision.

But why am I looking for all this outside?

From where? And why?

I know it very well that except me there is nothing that is mine.

There was once a clear pathway leading to the destination of life but it is lost and scattered.

Do you realise how it feels to see fresh, innocent dew drops transformed to tears! A world that was fragrant once is getting choked and suffocated.

A revolution, once complete in itself is dying a slow torturous death.

A thought that would be renewed and rejuvenated with each new year, getting stale and worn out like the concept of God.

A dawn is moving towards dusk without a fragrant noon.

A deep vision is feeling lost and blinded in the crowd.

7th January, 1968 Jeeti

from imroz

95

Maja,

A man was caught while looking through the window, he was trying to make a painting of God.

His self portrait was torn and flung around his neck and he was exiled for life in his own self.

The Jesus of the Church came down from the cross, humming and wearing his clothes, he peered outside. And there - in the darkness of the day he saw an entire world hung on the cross, fully clothed, open mouthed but silent.

Since God has been immersed in the Ganges, people are not dying any more.

But paintings, poems and art die everyday.

8th January, 1968 Jeeti

95

from imroz

Maja,

The desire to live my life my own way has alienated me and I am intensely lonely in this crowded city.

Two of your letters joined my loneliness today.

I have not been able to find a room or a house. I am wandering here and there like a homeless destitute.

Even when I get a house, I am living like a gypsy. I have yet to find the land that makes me live in the real sense.

Maja! People like you and me remain homeless even while living in these houses, these cities and these countries. The land where we can live happily still lies, in our thoughts, in our creations, in our existence.

This search is the symbol of our homelessness.

This world of films lives and breathes in an alien land. Life here is uncertain and unsure. This fear is eating up vision, of the inhabitants of this land, their thoughts, their values and their creations appear hollow and eroded. We see the product of this fear every day.

Each colour of mine, each word of yours, is a quest. We resist incompleteness. One facet of this resistance, this quest this struggle is 'Naagi' — a nod to the struggle of your words and my lines.

10th January, 1968

Jeeti

96

from imroz

Maja,

The canvas of yesterday is still like a night, sad on the easel of the sky.

The colours, scattered like the stars are finding their own direction.

The time, contrary to its disposition, appears helpless and is getting confined and shrunk within its bounds like a frame.

With tired feet and tired mind, I and my brush are walking slowly along.

13th January, 1968 Jeeti

from imroz

98

Aashi,

The present time is more of a curse.

Spring is slowly eroding the tree of life, through its own leaves, its own flowers.

14th January, 1968 Jeeti

from imroz

99

Hai o rbba nahion lagda dil mera.

Coming from Reshma's throat, my voice is traversing all over the desert.

If your city is also a part of this desert then you must have heard my voice.

The proofs of 'The Black Rose' are there in front of me.

The history of my wandering voice in the desert.

Not the entire history, just a few chapters.

The chapters that are still to be written, they are with you, with me and with Reshma.

8th February, 1968 Your Ami

from imroz

100

My Zorbi!

Since last night I am full of Khalil Gibran.

The writer who had awakened the man inside me eleven years ago in Andretta.

With remarkable simplicity and ease, he talks about everyone while talking about himself.

Love is the only freedom in this world.

28th September, 1968 Imroz

from imroz

101

Imma!

Bring some colours of holi in your brush this time.

I swear by my pale and colourless hands....

9th February, 1968

from imroz

102

My life Jeeti!

Such loving and sweet letters! I feel like believing in life.

In a world, that is full of deceptions - you, your existence and your letters are a blessing. Otherwise life is a long accursed journey.

Who can know this better than the two of us.

The language department of Patiala has sent a cheque of a hundred and twenty five rupees.

They call it a "reward" but I call it an insult, rather a mockery. I could not keep this token of audacity on my table. So I spent Seventy Five paisa from my pocket and sent the cheque back through registered post.

Now the room is looking neat and clean with just your letters and my poems around.

Last evening, Devinder brought a copy of 'Screen'. My eyes located your design from a distance.

6th April, 1968 Maja

from imroz

103

My Jeeti,

While I was asleep in the afternoon I heard a knock at the door.

In a semi-wakeful state, I thought Jeeti would open the door and went back to sleep.

Someone knocked again and again.

I woke up but could not understand why you were not opening the door.

Mystified, I went towards your room to find the reason.

I was shocked to find the room vacant. After a while, it dawned on me that you were in Bombay.

On the fifteenth afternoon, Kandla came home. She took leave for three or four days otherwise she would have come on the nineteenth. She read my letter and came, dunking that mama is alone.

In the afternoon today a few Japanese ladies came to see batik. They bought things worth five hundred.

My wallet is full at the moment. And my heart is full too.

But I am your Zorbi and I swear by your work that I will not be sad.

17th September, 1968 Your Zorbi

from imroz

104

Jeeti!

The vegetables that you bought before leaving have finished, and so has the fruit.

There is nothing left in the fridge.

Even my life seems vacant – the number of breaths that you left, seem to be finishing.

Jeeti please don't get sad reading all that I have written.

It was written on a dark and lonely night.

Yes I am sad, but I am Zorbi. When I think about your work, I try and console myself.

I do not know if this is because of my declining years or just a feeling that life is transitory and only a few days are left.

Jeeti, if you really think there is some future in Bombay, you must struggle but do not wander aimlessly. A simple meal at home is also full of satisfaction when we are together.

I am talking like an eighty year old lady or a lady of the previous centuries.

May be that is what a perennial woman is like.

29th September, 1968 Forever, Maja

from imroz

105

My Religion! My honour!

When I think about you, an old and stale word like religion starts sounding fresh.

Your letters?

I feel where Geeta, Quran, Granth and Bible stop, your letters begin...

Avtar came and stayed with me for two-three days. She left last evening. She saw the sketch of Khalil Gibran on my table and asked, "Is this Inderjeet's sketch"?

I felt good.

She mistook Khalil Gibran for you.

Features could differ but thoughts are the real resemblance. Honestly after reading your letter I felt that your face and that of Khalil Gibran have merged.

There is something sacred that I have seen in you.

I have read about that in books but have never seen it on any familiar face.

Since you left I have written a poem, an article and a story. But all these are my scanty and frugal wages.

The actual reward of my life is you, my Imroze.

When will you come home!

Tell me a date so that I can start counting the days on my finger tips.

My fingers will appear dear to me.

6th October, 1968 Your Zorbi

from imroz

106

Immu!

The city that fills your hands with work, I revere that city. Yesterday was Nagmani evening.

Broke a coconut and a piece of jaggery too.

But, first I touched a piece to your memory.

Around eighteen people were there.

It was a good evening, serious and solemn.

Shailu has not come till now.

I get startled with every little noise, go and check the door again and again.

This is happening since the fifteenth.

In panic I sent him a telegram yesterday. But no reply has come so far.

His friend, Miss Stalin rings up time and again to ask about him.

She asks me "he hasn't even written a letter?" And I ask her, "has he not written to you also?"

There is a gap of one generation between us – but a woman is a woman, whether a mother or a beloved.

I met some Russian people who have come for the Nehru Prize. Mariam came home three or four times, she gave me two Russian poems for Naagmani.

Both the poems are very sweet and moving. I have already translated one. She has also given a picture of the poet.

I shall meet the German representative tomorrow and note the correct German pronunciation of some words, before giving the work to the press.

I have received a letter from Germany saying that they like the book of short stories "After the war", a book of German poems should also be published.

I will think about it next year.

This year I am tired after translating these twenty five stories.

I have located the Delhi office of South Africa.

They have written to the London office for a portrait of Richard Raive.

They want to come home to meet me.

18th November, 1968 Your Zorbi

from imroz

107

My Immva!

You are my permanent address and I am yours.

Your letter that I received today made me feel that you are not getting mine.

This is really unfair.

I sent off your daughter* in the morning today. Your room is looking like the courtyard of a fathers house from where the daughter has just departed - relieved but vacant.

Shailu called. He will come on 25th night.

He was singing "'Jan-gan-man" on the telephone.

Listening to his voice, I had an idea. The Navyug people are asking me to write an epic poem on Guru Nanak.

I don't think I would write that.

However, a thought came to my mind - when Tripta was pregnant (Nanak's mother-to-be), what would she be dreaming.

I wanted to write those dreams and the tide of the poem should be "Garbhvati".

---

* She referred to 'Naagmani' as my daughter. She wrote this letter after the release of an edition.

With a son like Nanak in the womb, her dreams must be really sweet.

21st Novemeber, 1968 Your Zorbi

from imroz

108

My jeeti,

Shelley has brought some really good books.

The one that I am reading now is 'The True Believer' by Eric Hoffer. You will also like it. He has remarkable clarity of thought.

Shelley really fills the evening.

He talks only about books and I can talk about books till doomsday.

It is afternoon now.

Shelley is playing music records in his room and Miss Stalin is sitting with him.

You are with me each moment.

29th November, 1968 Your Zorbi

from imroz

109

My Imma!

Just saw your work - the creation of your hands, and felt as if I have met you.

I have "Shadows of the Past" in front of me.

The postman brought this book just now.

I cannot take my eyes off its tide.

I can see more of your face on the tide than mine... many salutes to your talent.

And listen!

In the poem that I have written today, Tripta bows in front of her own womb.

The womb symbolises those hands that are capable of creating someone like Nanak.

I bow to your hands, your creative hands. For any artist, the hands are the womb.

The postal strike finished on the 21st. So I took Naagmani to the post office. They told me that they would accept it but suggested that it should not be posted today. There was so much of backlog to be cleared that the workers would not be able to handle everything simultaneously, so they are just tearing up newspapers and magazines and suggested that I should give them a call on Monday – and if the situation is normal then I should post Naagamani.

So now on 23rd I have posted Naagmani.

At the moment my body is full of sweat - one because of heat and sunshine and the other because of your absence and I am totally drenched in both.

Your Zorbi, Your Ami, Your Maja, Your Binna.

It is such a strange feeling, Shelley's first wages are now on my palm.

During his holidays, he made a proposal for someone for eighty rupees, four rupees were deducted for the board and seventy six were given.

On his way back, he bought a packet of Regent cigarette for Rs. 3 for me and Rs. Seventy three in cash.

He gave me his earnings in the afternoon.

In the evening I got your letter.

Both my palms are rich today.

28th December, 1968 Your Zorbi

I am all alone here feeling like a helpless child who has been abandoned by his mother.

Woe to the trains that are not bringing you back.

Totally furious, Zorbi

Gulzar came yesterday... "Came to know that you are not feeling well, what is the matter".

I replied, "I am fine but the pain begins in the evening, as the sun sets.

Gulzar started laughing, "In ancient times someone had tied 'time' to the bed. You should tie the sun and do not let it set." And I told him "I have tied the sun, when Jeeti's letter comes in the evening, my sun rises."

Honestly Jeeti!

Each letter of yours is the evening sun.

Am I not capable of miracles?

I have tied the sun.

3rd January, 1969 Waiting for you with each breath – Zorbi

from imroz

111

Imma!

If I get to live with you, one lifetime will not be enough?

It is Sunday today and it is freezing cold and there is severe pain in my shoulders.

The darkness of the twilight has chilled my bones, and then I received your letter, it has intensified the feeling that life is so ephemeral.

“She” lived a thousand years, waiting to meet her beloved. But I am that “she” who wants to live a thousand years after meeting you.

I am not feeling too well these days.

It was Krishan Chander evening yesterday. Gulzar took me in his car and dropped me back too. Revati Saran wanted that I should greet Krishan on the stage for a while. So I just spoke for two minutes. Dr. Zakir Hussain was presiding over the function.

You know what I said?

I spoke in Urdu:

Tune dekhi hai wo peshani, wo rukhsar, wo hont
Zindagi jinke tassavur mein luta di hamne.

You have seen the brow, the bearing, the lips,
we have spent a life time in this imagination.

This couplet by Faiz was written for the rival in love.

I think all of us who love the written word are "love rivals". We know this pain all too well and we know why we just give our lives away. Krishan is a dear friend and a dear love rival too. Today I want to give him the greatest compliment, "we his love-rivals salute him and wish him good health from the deepest recesses of the heart."

At the moment I am not feeling well at all and I am writing this from my bed.

This letter is like my arm — nine hundred miles long arm extended towards you.

Maja

Shelley | Imroz | Candy

Naagi

12th January, 1969 Your Zorbi

from imroz

112

Jeeti,

Is there any wall in the world where I can hang this portrait? I cannot find a single one that is complete and unbroken.

There are cracks and dampness in the walls of this world. Even God is not a good architect.

Whenever I meet someone, I become all the more lonely.

Each meeting, each connection strongly reinforces my loneliness.

Earlier everybody was unhappy with you and with me, now Shelley and Naagi have also joined us. Miss Stalin's mother is unhappy with Shelley and the world of Punjabi literature, with Naagi.

Whenever I call at the office of the publisher for the new issue of Naagmani, I always get a rude reply. I wanted Naagmani to be ready by the nineteenth but got the reply, "Heavens will not fall if the magazine is not ready by evening."

The content was more than the required limit, so I told the publisher that the last article should definitely be included even, if we have to add another page and we could reduce a page from the poems. And the reply was, "So what if the last article is not published, it is not going to change the face of the world as such." It was a very rude and irritated voice.

Sometimes I feel I should install a machine in my bedroom, compose and print on my own.

Even Mr. Jain, the paper merchant - I called him up at least fifteen times – but he came on the line just once and every other time I left a message that he should call back.

He never did.

He never calls back.

The envelopes are still not ready.

I am thinking of Balzac today.

He also went through similar circumstances - when he was driven to the wall by publishers he became the writer and the publisher himself and then he had enough of paper problems and he opened his own paper factory.

And now I am!

It is time to become the creator oneself.

The entire world should be destroyed and new one needs to be created.

15th January, 1969 Zorbi

from imroz

113

A POSTCARD

In your absence, I feel my own self is also absent from life.

Go to a homeopath today and tell him to give you some concoction so that you rush back home immediately.

O my God

Your Reshma

Iima!

I keep imagining a leafy cottage on the Juhu beach.

At times I feel I want to wind up everything here – all the bills and taxes that have to be paid bother me so much. Received the water bill just now, car insurance is also due and even the house tax. I have the responsibility of Naagmani and have to deal with the moods of the press people. Why can't we stop doing all this.

I would be happy living in a small cottage, happily, growing leaves and flowers, watering plants, and cooking simple meals twice a day.

I do not want fame or money.

Just want to be with flowers, bloom like them and then fade away quietly.

I just want to live a peaceful life, cook simple meals with whatever you bring home.

23rd July, 1971 Maja

from imroz

115

Imma!

Thank God!

Each morning your letter arrives without which the world would not really be worth living.

I had to go for T.V. recording today. When I went there I realised that Harbhajan was there with all his instruments.

I had been reading Kazan at home, Greek passion and the scene was a total contrast over there.

But thank God when I returned, I got your letter - pure and beautiful like the heart of Kazan Zakis.

So I just shook off the dust of a hundred paths that had settled on me and read your letter and was in my elements again.

This time you will have to come back soon.

You also have to prepare for Europe and when we come back we shall stay in Mumbai.

11th july, 1972 Your Ami

from imroz

116

O my Imma!

If ever I have to live without you, I would say no to God also. I refuse to live a deprived life.

If living is deducted out of life then I am not interested in what remains.

Your phone call at night infused new life in me.

Europe is not important.

If Bombay is able to give us a future, it is enough for us.

19th July, 1972 Maja

O my Imma!

Today Shelley has gone to Patiala for two or three days.

My loneliness has deepened all the more.

Shapeless and formless like the Roman Empire.

H.G. Wells writes that the Roman Empire kept on expanding, like an unplanned novel and then collapsed suddenly.

This loneliness will also collapse once and for all, when you come back home.

27th July, 1972 Your Ami

from imroz

118

Imma!

I kept your room closed yesterday.

Felt restless and nervous and opened it today.

But a silence seems to have spread all over the floor and has reached the ceiling.

15th April 1974

Your Ami

from imroz

119

Imma!

Let me tell you something interesting today.

Devinder had come yesterday. He was telling about an Urdu poet whom he met at the radio station. He asked him to help him borrow three thousand rupees from Amrita Pritam as he had heard that Amrita is very helpful.

Navraj was sitting close by.

He said, "Devinder Uncle! Tell him to speak in hushed tones. If Indira Gandhi hears him, she might just nationalise Amrita Pritam."

It is Monday today and the sun has just risen.

When it goes a little high, your letter will come.

I do not know when would I hear your voice and the sound of your footsteps coming up stairs.

27th May, 1974 Your Maja

from imroz

120

Imma!

Life is really meaningless.

I think I am the victim of my own idealism.

Whatever I have thought and written, does it have any meaning in the world?

I am reading Gulag Archipelago, a terrible piece of history.

At times I get up in the middle of the night and the darkness engulfs my being. And then this strange month of December as if we have to pay some debts of life - the installments of income tax, road tax, Insurance and the compulsory deposits.

We work so hard for a living, pay our taxes honestly, even give a headcount of every little article in the house, and still there is no security of the future!

Now I do not even feel like writing.

All my life I have lived in the false illusion of an inherent goodness of humanity.

I have even asked people to live in this hope.

What has really come out of all this writing? Has the world improved? Absolutely wrong, nothing will happen......

And yes about the film – if Basu doesn't even remember the context then I will not come to Bombay just to remind him.

I am very tired.

So much of my work has gone waste, let this also go the same way.

I have no complaints and no hopes.

14th June, 1975 Maja

from imroz

121

My Imma,

There was a trunk call from Chandigarh, informing that the Punjab Government wants to make a film on the "contribution of women to the history of Punjab".

It will be made by Pooja Kapoor and director Bharti and I have been asked to write a synopsis and send it to the government.

Pooja will make the film if the synopsis is approved.

I have declined to write the script on this condition of approval. I cannot write anything for the files of the government and for the "enlightened members" of the committee.

Already I have had enough of it with the F.F.C.

I want to spend the remaining days of life just with myself and with you and with some beautiful books.

5th December, 1975 Your Maja

from imroz

122

Imma!

A strange thing happened last night.

I was reading Gulag Archipelago till late in the night. The first chapter is about an arrest – how in the middle of the night, suddenly a knock on the door is heard and an innocent man is arrested.

He keeps on asking "Me"?

"But why?"

He never gets a reply.

Instead he is thrown in the dungeon for 20 years or shot dead in the darkness outside.

And I dreamt that there was a knock at our door and the police arrested Darji.

In my dream Darji was still alive and in the morning I came to know that they shot him dead

What could be the significance of this dream?

Is it that the death of millions of innocent people touched me and shook me so badly that it was equivalent to my fathers death?

Or is it that Darji actually did not die a natural death?

It was not in my sight and I do not know how he died.

But this thought never came to my mind all these years.

You know, after Darji died, that boy Gian Singh, forged his signature and sold his land.

Who knows, his death might be a mystery that I have never known.

It was a strange dream

28th December, 1975 Maja